Other Books by Author
Derek Slaton

Dead Texas Series

1. Day Zero
2. No Comfort
3. Lonesome Road
4. The Journey West

Direct to VHS Series

1. Butcher of Camp Barlow

Grindhouse Chronicles Series

1. Smoothen Silky: Demon Fighting Pimp
2. Midget with a Chainsaw
3. Curse of the Blue Diablo (Double Feature with Pestilence A-Go-Go)
4. Smoothen Silky vs The WereCougar

More information can be found at

www.GrindhouseChronicles.com

ELIMINATOR TIME FORCE
By Derek Slaton
© 2018

CHAPTER ONE

"Look man, I don't care what you have to do. Either get me the stuff you owe me, or you are going to end up the same way Marco did." Kevin Hauser sneered into his burner phone.

"I… I can get it to you on Monday. Yeah… Monday. I… I just need a little more time," the frightened voice on the other end stuttered.

Kevin resisted the urge to throw the phone onto the dash of his 1987 Oldsmobile Cutlass Supreme. He had spent years and an ungodly amount of money retrofitting the classic from the ground up. Spinner rims, ground effects, and a fresh coat of jet black paint would have made the car stand out in the best of neighborhoods, let alone on Kevin's street—which had more bars on the windows than the prison he spent eight months in for assault.

"You are really trying my patience man. I don't like it when people waste my time, and I guarandamn-tee you aren't going to like me when I lose my patience," Kevin said as he slowly pulled into his driveway. The volume of his voice resonated along the quiet street, causing his next door neighbor to draw the blinds shut.

"Okay, I hear you sir… and I promise-"

"Save your promises for someone who will believe them," Kevin cut in, freezing in place at the sight of his front door hanging open.

He lowered the phone, the voice on the other end yammering empty platitudes. Incompetence was always something that angered him, but paled in comparison to someone breaking into his home.

He squeezed the cheap phone so tightly that audible cracks reverberated through the night air. "Just get it done or pay the price," he said with finality and tossed it on the passenger seat.

Kevin rummaged around in the center console for his butterfly knife. The powder blue handled blade was a gift from his mother after he was released from prison. In his line of work, he needed protection, but carrying a gun was a risky prospect for someone with a parole officer who had an annoying habit of being thorough with the checkups.

He approached the door cautiously, juggling open the blade as he composed himself. He tried to assess the situation by peering through the curtains. There was a lamp illuminated in the front corner of the living room, highlighting the silhouette of someone sitting on the couch by the window.

After a short pause on the porch, Kevin burst into the front room blade first, letting out a battle cry in the process. He stomped through the middle of the room, pausing at the doorway to the kitchen before turning to face the trespasser. Kevin pointed the knife towards the floor when he saw a young woman in her early twenties sitting on the couch reading a magazine with one hand and drinking a beer with the other.

She looked like any one of a thousand other girls that might be found in a college town. Her athletic build fit her five foot six inch frame well; and made it pretty evident she was familiar with CrossFit. The shoulder length brown hair was pulled into a ponytail and showed she was more concerned with functionality rather than appearance. Her *Iron Maiden Caught Somewhere in Time* t-shirt, however, alerted the world she did in fact have great taste in music.

"Who the fuck are you?" Kevin asked with a mixture of bemusement and anger.

She kept her head down and continued to read her magazine, holding up her beer hand as a non-verbal *hold on*.

"Are you kidding me right now?" He snapped, the amusement gone from his voice. "You have to the count of five before I slice you up."

She closed the magazine and gently set it beside her.

"One," he warned.

She raised her chin. "My apologies, that was rude of me."

"Two." His voice rose ever-so-slightly.

"It was a great article on Bruce Dickinson and how he's a certified airline pilot," she continued casually.

"Three," he snarled, cracking his neck in preparation for the assault.

"Imagine being that famous, touring eight months out of the year, and the way you relax is flying jumbo jets with hundreds of passengers," she said before taking a long sip of beer. "Simply amazing."

"Four!" he yelled, spittle flying off his bottom lip.

"You know, you may want to think long and hard about your next word," she warned and finished off the beer. "You may not like what happens when you get there."

"FIVE!" Kevin screamed before lunging at her.

The beer bottle hit him in the face, momentarily stunning him. Before he could recover, she leapt off the couch and disarmed him by grabbing his wrist with one hand and delivering a powerful uppercut to his elbow with the other.

He stumbled backwards with a high-pitched yelp in an octave typically audible only to dogs. "I'm gonna kill you!"

She swooped down to pick up the fallen blade, and flipped it around a couple times with her left hand like a seasoned pro. She raised two fingers in a *come hither* motion, smirking all the while.

He yelled and swung hard with a straight jab. She met his punch with the business end of the blade, imbedding it deep within his fist. Kevin staggered away from her, unable to even vocalize his pain. He stumbled about for a moment before regaining his footing, just in time for her to move in for the kill, launching herself knee-first into his chest.

The force of the blow sent Kevin flying backwards, hitting the floor hard. She followed him down, knees pressing into his biceps and effectively pinning him.

"Told you that you should have thought about your next word," she teased, and tapped him on the forehead.

He tried in vain to swing at her with his knife hand. On the second attempt, she grabbed his wrist and pulled the blade out, sending a spatter of blood onto the wall. He continued to flail his arms until she pressed the knife into his trembling throat.

"Whoa whoa whoa, easy now honey, let's talk about this," Kevin begged.

She raised an eyebrow. "Oh, so *now* you want to talk? What, no more counting?"

"Nope. No more counting," he assured her. "Look, if you want the stash, it's under a false bottom in the cabinet beside the stove."

"Don't care about your stash," she said, pressing harder against his flesh. "I do, however, care about the keepsakes from the three women you've murdered. Not to mention the four other women you have on your hit list."

He laughed nervously. "What in the world are you talking about? I never-"

She cut him off by smashing his nose with the butt of the knife. "Believe me when I say that I'm the last person you would ever be able to lie to," she said.

"I'm telling you, you have the wrong person," he pleaded.

She held three fingers in front of his face. "Marcie Davis, Elaine Woodman, Leigh Smith."

Kevin's face drained of all of its remaining color.

"You stalked all three of them for weeks before following them home from their bartender jobs on sixth street," the woman said, voice a low husk. "Once they crashed out from a long night slinging drinks, you broke into their homes, raped them, then slit their throats and gleefully watched as they bled out.

"But you weren't finished. Rather than let them die with dignity, you packed them into the trunk of your car and drove them out to Grant State Park. Once there you dumped the bodies in a secluded area known for its high concentration of feral hogs, which I have to admit is a great way to dispose of a corpse. Frankly I'm shocked that someone of your limited mental capacity could come up with an idea like that on your own."

"Alright, so you think you know some things," he replied shrilly. "But I know for a fact you ain't got no proof. Because if you did this place would be swarming with cops, and I don't see no blue lights!"

She laughed. "Wait, you think I'm a cop?"

"It's either that or you are with some rival gang trying to

blackmail me to get in on my territory. In which case," he said with a
sneer, "they shoulda just sent your
fine ass over as a peace offering—I
would have been happy to share."

"Wow, you sound really cocky
for a man with no functioning hands
and a knife to his throat," she
said. "Are you really such a deluded
alpha male that you don't realize
your life is about to end?"

He scoffed. "Oh give me a
break. Yeah you fucked me up pretty
good, but I know lots of bitches
like you that will throw down. We
both know you ain't got the balls
to—"

She drove the knife into his
throat and then pulled it out, leaving it on the floor beside him. His
eyes filled with dread he gasped for
air, gargling his words.

She wandered into the kitchen
and popped another beer as his body
went limp.

"Alright, time to get to work,"
she said, and knelt down to rip his
shirt. She reached into her back

pocket and pulled out a silver LED laser with a blue tip. "You know, you're lucky I'm rusty, or else I would have left you alive for this. But legibility is more important than your suffering."

As the smell of burning flesh filled the room, she made a series of hand motions and then sat back to admire her work. "Eh, not bad for freehand."

CHAPTER TWO

Artemis headed into her small one-bedroom apartment and tossed her pack on the kitchen table. She made her way past the makeshift cot on the floor and over to a small desk that was buried in papers, electronic parts, and a laptop that had been outdated since the turn of the century. It took her a moment of searching before she was able to locate a black dry erase marker.

To an outside observer, the wall beside her desk was reminiscent of a tin foil hat wearing conspiracy theorist's wall depicting his latest attempt to connect Elvis to the JFK assassination. Maps, surveillance photos, and bits of string interconnecting them all covered virtually all of the space. The only exceptions were three dry erase boards hung in the corner just above the desk.

Artemis licked her thumb and reached over to a small white board marked *SAVED*. She erased a number three and replaced it with a seven. She took a moment to admire the new count of sixteen thousand, two hundred and forty seven.

On the next board—marked *Most Wanted*, she drew a large black line through the name Kevin Hauser, who had been a new entry on the board at position ten. He joined several other names who had been marked off in recent weeks, but not Anthony Duke, who was at the very top and written twice as large as anybody else.

She shook her head and pursed her lips before taking a seat and opening the computer.

The laptop took a moment to boot up, giving Artemis a brief reprieve from the world. The moment was a fleeting one, as the screen greeted her with a bright red *Alert* notification.

The headline read *Child, Age 11, Found Strangled in Woods Behind Family Home*. She quickly scrolled through the story until she found the name of the kid, Benjamin Kimble. As she had feared, it matched a name on the third board, labeled *Prez*. There were a list of names and numbers starting at forty-eight and going through sixty, five of which had already been marked out.

"Son of a bitch," she muttered.

She grabbed the marker and scratched out number fifty-eight, Benjamin Kimble. Upon replacing the cap, she threw it against the desk where it landed with a soft thud on the reams of paper.

Artemis slumped down in her chair for a moment before picking up her cell phone and dialing Robert.

"Well, this can't be good," he greeted. "You never just call to say hello."

She shook her head. "Number fifty-eight just went down. Child strangled in the woods behind his house."

"You think it's the Duke again?" he asked.

"It matches his M-O, so it has to be. It's also the third future President that's been murdered in the last six weeks in the exact same way. That can't be a coincidence."

He clucked his tongue. "No, it can't be. You still think he's working with one of ours?"

"It's the only way to explain it, but it still doesn't entirely make sense," Artemis mused. "If he was working with one of ours then why would he only be taking out the initial presidents while leaving their replacements alone?"

"Who knows? Maybe they have damaged equipment and aren't getting updates. Or maybe they are just bored and want to remix the future. You know, get some different war movies and TV shows out of it," Robert suggested.

She laughed. "While I hope that's the case, I get the sense their motives are a bit more nefarious."

"I agree wholeheartedly. So have you made contact with the agent yet?"

"Left the message for him tonight. If all goes as planned

we'll be having breakfast at your place in the morning," Artemis replied.

"Just for the record, I'm still not completely sold on this plan."

She sighed. "I understand, but desperate times call for desperate measures."

"Yeah, I know," he agreed.

"See you in the morning."

"I'll be ready," Robert assured her, and there was a click as he ended the call.

Artemis tossed her phone onto the pile of papers on the desk. She stared through the news article for a beat, and clenched her jaw.

"I'm going to get this bastard," she hissed, and slammed the laptop closed.

CHAPTER THREE

A fleet of police vehicles con-
gregated outside the late Kevin
Hauser's house. Blue lights illuminated the neighborhood, which was
something of a regular occurrence in
these parts. So regular that not a
single neighbor left the comfort of
their home to investigate. This made
it a lot easier for Special Agent
Hodge to get to the heart of the
crime scene.

Hodge was a seasoned vet of the
force, and one of the few plain-
clothed officers in his precinct. He
walked up to the front door with the
swagger of an officer of the law.
His faded jeans and untucked button
down shirt made him more suited to
be pulling up a stool in a dive bar
than investigating a murder.

"Hey this is a crime scene pal,
you can't be in here," the officer
by the door barked.

He flashed his badge in return.
"I'm Special Agent Hodge."

"Really, *you're* Hodge?" the officer asked. "You don't look like much of a cop."

"Well I am, they gave me a badge and everything. Even let me carry a gun, but then again this is Texas so I guess that part doesn't make me so special," Hodge replied.

The officer shook his head in disgust. "You know, my mother always said it's important to take pride in the way one looks."

"Well, your mother was a smart woman," Hodge replied with a grin. "She knew you were an ugly child and couldn't withstand any other outward facing flaws if you were ever going to see a naked woman without paying a cover charge first."

The officer blinked at him in disbelief.

"Now are you going to tell me why I got called into this or would you like to continue discussing your mother's fashion tips?" Hodge snapped.

The officer squinted his eyes in displeasure before pointing towards the kitchen door. "Dead guy over there has your name written all over him."

The Special Agent walked over to Kevin's body. "Well, he wasn't wrong," he muttered as he knelt down to look at the corpse's mutilated chest. *Special Agent Hodge* had been burned into his upper torso, and a small arrow pointed down towards a USB stick resting on his stomach.

He took a plastic glove from his pocket and put it on before carefully picking up the USB stick to inspect it. "Somebody get me a laptop!" he called, and strode into the den.

The officer from the door dropped brought a laptop and slammed it down on the table in front of the couch with a little more force than was maybe necessary.

"Anything else, Special Agent Hodge?" he asked, voice dripping with disdain.

Hodge grinned. "Yeah, how about some coffee?"

"I'll send your server right out," came the snarky reply.

The Special Agent turned the USB stick over in his hands as the computer booted up.

"Alright, let's see what we got," he muttered as he plugged in the drive.

The desktop vanished, leaving on a black screen and a single line of white text that read *What Name Did Your Dad Originally Want For You?*

A blinking cursor awaited his answer.

"What the hell kind of question is that?" the officer asked, from over his shoulder.

Hodge pursed his lips. "It's a question that nobody should know the answer to outside of me and my father."

"So the killer is working with your father?"

"Only if they are psychic. My father has been dead for twenty years."

"Your mother?"

"Ten years," Hodge replied. He leaned back on the couch, stretching his hands out behind his head. "No, this… this is something else."

He contemplated for a moment before taking a position at the keyboard. He carefully typed out *Francis* and hit enter. The black screen faded away to reveal a secondary desktop page. The grey gradient background was broken up by a single video file in the middle of the screen. The file name read *For Special Agent Hodge ONLY.*

"I'm going to need some privacy," Hodge said, motioning for the officer to leave. Once the room was clear he double clicked the icon and the video began to play. There was a silhouette of a slender person with shoulder length hair in front of a dim orange glow.

"Special Agent Hodge." It was a woman's voice. "I realize that this isn't the ideal way for us to meet, but I figured it would be the only way for you to take me seriously. I have information regarding the mass murderer Anthony Duke that would be beneficial to your investigation."

Hodge nearly leapt out of his chair. *What the hell? Did someone hack my computer?* He had always been focused on Duke as the main suspect in those killings, but could never collect enough hard evidence to prove it. While he was one hundred percent convinced Duke was behind the murders, he never volunteered the name to anyone else in his department for fear of being kicked off the case. *Did they break into my office? Have they been stalking me? How does this woman know that name?*

"I will be at Tate's Bar tomorrow at nine AM. Ask for Artemis, and the bartender will point you in the right direction. If you bring back-up, I will be gone before you walk through the front door, and you will never get the information that I have. I look forward to meeting with you face to face." She leaned forward and reached for the camera, but paused. "Oh, and one more thing about our friend in the next room.

His name is Kevin Hauser. He is responsible for the rape and murders of Marcie Davis, Elaine Woodman, and Leigh Smith. Chances are all three of them are in your missing persons database as their bodies haven't been found yet.

"You might want to send a team over to Grant State Park to start looking. Have them concentrate on the areas where feral hogs congregate. His prints should match those found in all three of their apartments as well. And if that's not enough to convince you, take a peek under the false bottom in the cabinet beside the stove. You're welcome."

The video ended.

Hodge closed the laptop and took a deep breath before pulling out the USB key and pocketing it.

He headed into the kitchen and looked at the cabinet beside the stove. "Hey, any of your men gone through the cabinets in here?" Hodge yelled to the officer in the other room.

"Nope, we just cleared the premises for potential hostiles then waited for you to get here," the officer replied.

He reached into the cabinet and touched the bottom, freeing up a loose board and causing it to fall. It had a soft landing on a gallon freezer bag of blue meth that had been prepackaged into individual fun size portions. Another small bag was underneath it, containing three locks of hair. Each lock had a small label on them with the first name of the girls mentioned in the video.

Hodge's heart pounded in his ears as he strode back out to the living room. "Hey officer, are you on with Dispatch?"

"Yeah, what do you need?"

"I need three names run through missing persons. Marcie Davis, Elaine Woodman, and Leigh Smith," the Agent instructed.

"Got it," the officer said and grabbed his radio.

Hodge leaned against the cabinets and inspected the locks of hair. His mind raced to process what had just happened. *This guy wasn't even on our radar, but somehow she not only knew about it but took him out,* he thought. *Maybe she actually does know something about Duke.*

"Got the info on those girls," the officer said as he entered the kitchen. "All three of them were reported missing over the last four months."

Hodge contemplated for a moment before handing the bag of hair over. "Officer, how would you like to have your picture in the paper tomorrow?"

"What do you mean?"

"Well I'm pretty sure these locks of hair match the three girls you just asked dispatch about. And I'm also pretty sure that asshole in there is the reason they are on the missing person's list." He tossed the bag to the officer.

"What? Wait, this is your case," the officer protested.

"And I'm handing it over to you. I'm following up a much larger lead on a different case that takes priority."

His mouth opened and closed like a fish. "But… but… you can't!"

"Relax buddy, couple quick bits of advice. Never give the press details they don't need to know, always let the cutest reporter ask the first question, and make sure you do your mother proud by taking her advice to heart and dressing up in something spiffy," Hodge rattled off as he walked by the bewildered officer, slapping him on the shoulder as he went. "Oh, and one more thing, pretty sure the girls are in Grant State Park hanging with some feral hogs. You might not want to dress up for that part."

The Special Agent exited the house, pausing to take a breath in the cool night air. He had a thousand questions and zero answers, at least none that made any sense. For now, all he could do was hurry up and wait.

CHAPTER FOUR

Tate's Bar was an Austin south side legend, first opening its doors in January of 1971. Throughout the years every up and coming hard rock, punk and metal band imaginable had graced the eight by ten stage tucked away at the back of the venue, leaving their band signature on the wall before departing. Four decades later a patron, could relive the entire musical history of the building just by reading the names that had been left on every exposed surface. While considered a treat to die hard music fans, the residents of the nearby multi-million dollar condos were less impressed.

Hodge opened the ancient wooden front door, exposing the grime from the previous evening's show to an unhealthy dose of sunlight.

Before his eyes could adjust to the dimly lit room, a deep voice bellowed from behind the bar, "Morning!"

Hodge rubbed his eyes to accelerate the adjustment period. Eventually focused on a burly six foot two man standing behind the bar. "Morning," he greeted as he walked towards him and sat on the corner stool.

The bartender set out a surprisingly clean shot glass and poured some low level whiskey right to the brim. Hodge studied the glass for a moment, then looked the man right in the eye.

"Dude. It's nine in the morning," he said.

The man sighed and turned to the counter behind him for a coffee pot and mug. He stopped the pour two-thirds of the way up and dumped the whiskey in.

Hodge lifted the cup in a *cheers*. "Thank you, that's more like it."

"I aim to please," the man replied.

The Agent took a sip and then leaned on his elbow. "I'm looking for Artemis."

"Thank you for coming Special Agent Hodge," her familiar voice came from behind him.

He turned on his stool, careful not to spill his brew. "You aren't what I expected," he said.

"I bet you hear that a lot yourself," she replied, and motioned to the table next to her. "Please, have a seat. We have a lot to discuss."

"That we do," Hodge agreed, and slid into the seat across from her. "You killed a man and carved a message into his chest just to get my attention, so obviously I have a question or two for you."

Her eyes glinted with mischief. "Technically I burned a message into his chest. Carving is just too messy."

"Touche." He nodded.

She folded her arms in front of her on the table. "So. What would you like to know?"

"Well why don't we start at the top. Who are you?" He took another sip of his sharp brew.

She smiled wryly. "That's a bit of a loaded question. Do you want the short version or the long one?"

"Well I have a full cup of coffee and I'm in no hurry to get into the office, so might as well make it the long version," he said.

"Okay, my name is Artemis," she began, "I traveled back in time in order to make America a superpower and save it from a dystopian fate. After succeeding in that mission I started using my power and knowledge so that I can make the world a better place by taking out murderers before they are able to do harm. I reached out to you because I need your help in bringing down Anthony Duke, who I suspect is working with one of my former associates and is a threat to the future security of the nation and the world."

Hodge stared blankly at her for a moment before reaching down for his coffee cup. He rotated the mug a couple of times, giving him an opportunity to process everything that was just thrown at him. He took another long and slow sip.

"Okay." He took a deep breath. "I'll admit that I'm intrigued. I tell you what, I like a good sci-fi story as much as the next guy. How about you tell me about your dystopian future and how you managed to travel through time to save America while I finish my coffee? After that we'll go on a ride and I'll introduce you to some very nice people who will take great interest in what you have to say. They'll even give you a nice comfy room free of charge."

She nodded. "Good to see that you have an open mind, Special Agent Hodge."

"Yeah, let's go with that." He shrugged.

"The America I come from is very different than the one that exists in your timeline. At this point in my history, America only had around eighty-million people, and most of them were on the verge of starvation. Thanks to the global nuclear winter the majority of the crops were permanently destroyed. The only options for food were limited supplies that could be grown in greenhouses and underground, which wasn't a whole lot."

"Nuclear winter?" He furrowed his brow. "What, did the cold war turn out differently? Kennedy screw up the Cuban Missile Crisis?"

"There wasn't a cold war, at least not one with us involved." She shook her head. "World War Two was much more devastating for us. Germany was led by a competent military commander who was able to conquer Western Europe, and who was also smart enough to take out the Brits. Without England as a launching pad, there wasn't a D-Day, so America never entered the European front of the war. To make matters worse, the Nazis were able to completely control the Atlantic with their U-boats and captured Royal Navy ships. In order to protect our shores from invasion, we had to devote most of our ships to the east. The lack of firepower in the Pacific meant that after Pearl Harbor, we essentially battled Japan to a stalemate."

"So Germany never invaded Russia?"

"Nope, the military leaders were smart enough to know they'd never be able to survive a Russian winter with the military machinery they had," she continued. "So they solidified the lines right through the middle of Poland and both sides spent the next twenty-five years engaging in an unprecedented military buildup.

"There were numerous small level skirmishes in disputed territories, as well as a couple of proxy wars around the globe, but nothing major until 1982. A high level German government official was visiting a shared port town in Northern Poland where he was murdered by a drunk Russian soldier during a bar altercation. German leaders considered this an assassination.

"The Russians tried to appease them by doing a two day faux trial of the soldier resulting in his conviction and execution, but it was too late. Hardliners in the German government were able to convince the Chancellor that action had to be taken. By the end of the week there was a full scale ground war involving millions of troops on both sides. Details are spotty after that, but we do know that six months into the conflict, the nukes started flying. In a matter of hours dozens of cities and hundreds of millions of lives were snuffed out."

Hodge blinked at her, and then leaned back in his chair, giving her a light-hearted golf clap. "Well, bravo for preventing nuclear annihilation, but I still can't help but think you and your team did a rather poor job given that Hitler still came to power."

"Are you kidding me?" She slammed her fist down on the table. "Do you have any idea how many people we had to kill to make sure Hitler came to power?"

He gaped at her. "Wow, so your definition of a successful operation was to put one of the worst humans in history in charge?"

"In the simplest of terms, yes." She scoffed. "With the way things were left after World War One, there was going to be another massive conflict. Our mission was to create the conditions needed to put America in a position to be a world power, which we did."

He pursed his lips. "Yeah, just at the expense of forty million people."

"Forty million is a hell of a lot better than the billions lost as a result of the war and nuclear winter," she argued. "The USA alone lost forty million people due to starvation in the first year of the nuclear winter. God only knows how many people around the world died that year.

"Look, after World War One and the Treaty of Versailles there was going to be another major conflict with Germany leading the way. We did the best we could given the situation we were thrown in to. There were only eighteen of us and we had a limited amount of time to accomplish a near impossible task. We settled on Hitler because he was an incompetent leader, at least militarily. His actions led to the least destructive outcome for Europe and the world."

He put up a hand. "Wait, wait, I thought you had a time machine? Why wouldn't you give yourself decades to get things done?"

"Unfortunately, that's not the way time travel works." She cocked her head.

"Of course it isn't." He rolled his eyes. "Okay I'll bite. Explain to me how time travel works."

"Very well. In 2026 an alien space probe crashed into rural Texas-"

"Wait. Just, wait." Hodge scrubbed his hands down his face. "This story has time travel *and* aliens?" He downed the last of his coffee and thrust his cup into the air. "Barkeep! Can I get a refill? This feels like a two-cup kind of story."

Artemis cocked her head and smirked. "You good?"

"Oh yes, where were we?" He waved his hand in front of him. "Oh yeah, aliens in Texas. Please pro-ceed."

"America was in rough shape by 2026," she continued. "Famine and poverty were rampant, and virtually identical technologically to where we were in the mid-1980s. Every bit of our limited resources went into growing food. When the probe was an-alyzed, there was hope within the scientific community that it could be used as a power supply, so a top secret underground bunker was creat-ed for testing. The best and the brightest minds from across the country were assembled. Due to the secrecy and potential of the project we gave up our lives on the surface and took up permanent residence in the bunker. Despite our collective brilliance, we couldn't make any headway in harnessing the power of the alien artifact.

"That is until January of 2031. Out of nowhere the probe powered up, so our best tech went in to investigate. The power kept building for twenty minutes until it opened and emitted a blinding light. When we regained our eyesight, we saw that the tech had vanished."

"Let me guess, he went back in time?"

"Yeah, I did." The bartender said as he refilled Hodge's coffee. "All the way back to 1925."

The Agent blinked at him in amusement. "1925? Wow, you look really good for being a hundred and thirty years old."

He poured a shot of whiskey into the coffee before pouring one for himself and shot it back with a grin. "Thanks, I try to stay in shape."

"Oh man, that is amazing. So what, do you guys have some industrial strength botox in the future?"

Hodge shrugged, taking another sip of his fresh brew.

"They do actually," Artemis said. "According to the commercials, it's fantastic stuff. They inject some into a woman's face then bounce a quarter off of it so forcefully that it ricochets through a wall. However, that's not why we look so young."

He sighed and motioned for her to continue. "Do tell."

"We don't have anything scientific to back this up, but as best as we can tell the alien probe removed us from the timeline." She shrugged.

Hodge stared blankly at her for a moment. "What the hell does that even mean?"

"It means that we aren't impacted by time. In other words, we don't age," she explained.

He gaped. "So you are immortal?"

"No, we are still human and can be killed like any other person can," she replied. "Although, thanks to some future technology and medication we are a little more resilient than your average man on the street."

He took another slow deliberate sip. "Okay, so the the near immortal bartender got sent back to 1925. How could you possibly figure that out? Wouldn't your timeline be changed the moment he got here?"

"It did change, for everyone who wasn't in the complex," she explained. "Being in close proximity to the alien probe put us in a time protected bubble. We could see the changes happening around us, but weren't impacted by them."

He grinned. "So what did he do? Pull a Doc Brown and send you a telegram?"

"Well, it's kind of hard for Western Union to deliver to a top secret facility that is buried a mile underground, so he had to get a little more creative." She smiled. "Did you ever see the 1950s monster movie *Day of the Demon*?"

"Oh yeah, I loved that when I was younger." Hodge laughed. "Saw it at the drive-in on a double feature with *Lobster-Men from Mars*. What can I say, my father instilled me with a profound appreciation for the classics."

"Good," she said, and pointed to the bartender. "Now take a look at Robert over there. Does he look familiar to you at all?"

He turned and studied Robert, eyes narrowed and lips pursed. "You know, now that you mention it, he does look a lot like Doctor Roth, the archeologist that summons the demon."

"That's because he is," she declared.

"Get out!" He yelled, slamming his hand down on the table in excitement. "I gotta tell you Artemis, I'm thoroughly impressed with how much thought you have put into this whole performance here. Please, continue."

"Well, like you, I was raised with an appreciation of the classics, *Day of the Demon* included. The local TV station would play it every Halloween at midnight. Robert and I had an annual tradition where we would grab a six pack and watch it. That first year without him was rough, but when Halloween rolled around I wanted to carry on the tradition. When I tuned in that night I almost fell out of my chair when Robert came on screen."

Hodge's brow furrowed. "Wait, how did he manage to take over the role?"

"Well, when you fund a film it makes it a lot easier to get screen time," she replied.

"Let me guess, he pulled a Biff Tannen?" He took another deep gulp of coffee.

"You really like your *Back to the Future* references, don't you?"

"Well it's either that or *Terminator*, which now that I think about it, kind of describes you, doesn't it?" He raised an eyebrow in amusement.

"Not exactly," Artemis replied. "I'm just here to make the world a better place, not save some suburban waitress so she can fulfill her destiny."

He shrugged with a bewildered chuckle. "Fair enough."

"But yes, you are correct, he did pull a Bif Tannen," she continued. "Robert was a huge baseball fan, so he was able to amass quite a fortune early on."

"And he was able to use those ill-gotten gains to turn himself into a movie star. Brilliant."

"He thought so," Artemis said, giving Robert a little salute. He raised his glass in response.

Hodge turned his attention back on her. "Okay, so I get how he was able to let you know you had a time machine, but it still doesn't explain why you didn't have much time to alter the war. I mean going back to 1925 would give you plenty of time, wouldn't it?"

"You are correct, going back to 1925 would have given us plenty of

48

time," she agreed. "Unfortunately, that's not how it works. When activated, the alien probe sends people back exactly 106 years into the past. And because we don't have any control over it, we had to wait for the probe to power up on its own."

"And let me guess, it takes a while for that to happen," he cut in.

She nodded. "Five years, three weeks, six days and fourteen hours to be precise. My team and I arrived in 1930, and it took us two months to get to Germany. That didn't give us a lot of time to start eliminating the people we needed to."

Hodge downed the last of his coffee and wiped a drop from the corner of his mouth. "You know, I have to hand it to you, that was one hell of a story," he admitted. "I almost started to believe that you were a part of some sort of eliminator time force that came here to save humanity. You should be proud because you were that convincing. And finding a lookalike for Doctor

Roth from *Day of the Demon*, my god that was priceless. But I'm afraid that my cup is empty, so it's time to go find you a nice comfy room at the asylum."

Artemis leaned back in her chair, seemingly relaxed about the whole thing. "So you aren't interested in finding Anthony Duke?"

"Oh, I'm very interested," he said, "I just don't have any confidence you can help me. It's one thing to listen to a crazy alien time travel story over a cup of coffee. It's another thing entirely to go on a wild goose chase."

She nodded. "Fair enough. So what will it take for you to believe me?"

"You can use your crystal ball and tell me where Anthony Duke is." He rolled his eyes.

"I wish it were that easy, but he has fallen off the grid and I can't get a solid read on his whereabouts. That's why I contacted you, I need your help," she explained.

He sighed. "Well that's convenient. So you have nothing then?"

Robert dropped a file folder in
front of Hodge, and set a full mug
of coffee beside it. "This should do
the trick," he said, and then headed
back to the bar.

Hodge took a sip of his fresh
coffee and inspected the folder.
"Thank you, sir," he called over his
shoulder. "So tell me, Artemis, what
do we have here?"

"You have the information on
the murder of Anna Page, who will be
found dead tomorrow by a couple of
hikers," she said.

He pursed his lips. "So you
have tomorrow's headlines."

"Keep going, there's more," she
urged.

He flipped through the printouts before pausing on a headline
from 2020. "Wow, nice Photoshop work
there. You even redesigned the news-
paper's logo."

"Not Photoshopped, just print-
ing out the real news story," she
replied.

He made a noncommittal noise and ran his finger down the page. "Okay, let's see here. So Dan Bankston murdered Anna, along with six other women between now and when he is caught in 2020?"

"Yep, today is his first kill," she confirmed. "He picks his victims from internet dating sites, focusing on the women who enjoy camping. They go out on a few dates before he gets them to go out into the wilderness with him. Once they get out to the woods he spikes their drink before he and couple of low life scumbag friends rape and murder her."

He raised his eyebrows at her expectantly. "And what, you think these printouts prove you can see into the future?"

"On their own? No." She shook her head. "But when we go out to the woods and catch the trio in action, you'll know I'm legit."

Hodge reached down to his waistband for a pair of handcuffs and tossed them onto the table. "Give me one good reason why I should go along with this instead of arresting you right now?"

"Well for starters, you saw what I did to Kevin Hauser, and in the back of your mind you know it's way too early in the morning for that kind of struggle," she said. "However I'll cut you a break. Why don't you go ahead and cuff me?" She held her wrists out to him. "The woods are on the way to the asylum, so we can stop and investigate my claim. Worst case scenario you get a little exercise. Best case, you stop an innocent woman from needlessly dying. And besides, what else do you have to do today?"

Hodge leaned back in his chair, contemplating the offer before downing the last of his java.

"Oh what the hell," he muttered. He slammed his cup down and scooped up the cuffs. "I could probably use some time to recover from this coffee before heading into the office anyway. Great stuff by the way." He waved to Robert.

The bartender smiled. "I aim to please."

Artemis stood patiently with her arms stretched out in front of her while Hodge cuffed her.

Once she was secure, he motioned towards the door. "After you, ma'am."

She curtsied. "Such a gentleman. We'll be back in a bit, Robert."

The bartender waved at them. "You two kids have fun."

CHAPTER FIVE

Despite being one of the fastest growing metro areas in the country, Austin Texas had easy access to a wide variety of hiking trails and camping sites. Properly groomed and well maintained, these trails were visited by hundreds of thousands of people every single year and were one of the big draws to the city. Unfortunately for Artemis and Hodge, Mr. Bankston picked a campsite far off the beaten path.

"Okay, you have another half mile and then we are turning back," Hodge wheezed, struggling to catch his breath.

His cuffed hiking partner grinned. "You know, I would have thought a special agent who spends his days chasing down the baddest of the bad would be in better shape."

"Yeah, well, lucky for me tracking down the *baddest of the bad* is mostly research. I'm at a point in my career where I can delegate the actual chasing of bad guys," he huffed.

She shook her head. "Don't worry, it should just be up ahead here."

The two of them approached a clearing and knelt down about fifty yards short behind a downed tree. The Agent pulled out a pair of mini-binoculars to investigate the scene. There was a young couple sitting together on a blanket, giggling together.

"Well I'll be damned," he muttered as he sat down beside his companion. "There they are. A nice happy couple outside enjoying nature for some reason."

She raised an eyebrow. "Not a fan of the woods I take it?"

"Nope. I just never understood the appeal of shunning thousands of years of progress. Give me cold beer and indoor plumbing any day."

"Nothing wrong with that," she replied. "You should have seen the conditions I had to grow up in before moving to the secret facility.

It's a wonder I ever go outside these days."

"Okay, so now what?" he asked as he peered through the binoculars again. "I don't see anything particularly bad going on, outside of their drink choice. Man, life is just too short to waste it on cheap alcohol."

"It shouldn't be long," Artemis said. "Dan's MO was to pre-spike the beer and put a fresh cap back on the bottle so his victim wouldn't be suspicious. By the time she gets halfway through the poor girl is going to be borderline comatose."

Hodge sighed and made himself comfortable. "Can I ask you a question?"

She shrugged. "Sure."

"Why me?"

"What do you mean?" She stretched out on the ground, using a downed tree as a makeshift headrest.

He threw up his hands. "I mean why of all the law enforcement people in this town did you approach *me*?"

"Because you were simultaneously stubborn yet open minded," she
said.

He raised a confused eyebrow.
"That literally makes no sense."

"Sure it does," she argued. "I
read up on your pursuit of Duke.
Took you ten years to track him
down, but you never gave up. You
didn't care about accolades or pro-
motions—your only desire was to see
him behind bars. You never dismissed
any potential lead, even if it came
from a prostitute, drug dealer, even
a psychic."

"Wait, wait," he cut in, shaking his head, "when did I consult a
psychic?"

"Two years from now," she explained. "She approached you, claim-
ing to know where one of Duke's victims was buried. Everyone else in
the department laughed in her face,
but you took the time to listen to
her. You even went so far as to follow the lead she gave. Ultimately
there wasn't anything there, but
that didn't matter. You were willing

to believe someone most would deem insane, just on the off chance they were right. Gave me hope that you would believe me."

He shrugged. "Well, you aren't wrong. I mean, I'm in the middle of the woods spying on a couple of sex crazed teenagers through binoculars like a common perv because I think it might lead me to Duke. But how would you have known about that? Somehow I doubt that would have made the news."

"When you finally caught Anthony Duke, you got an enormous amount of press," she said. "You do a lot of interviews that delve into your career, the case, and even your past. How do you think I found out about Francis?"

He winced. "Oh lord, please don't call me that."

"Why not?" She grinned. "I think it's a testament to just how much your mother loved you. Hell it's a wonder she didn't pack you up and run."

"Yeah, I'd like to think naming
a son Francis would be sufficient
grounds for divorce," he said with a
chuckle, and then pursed his lips.
"Hey, heads up, I think we got something."

Anna wavered, and then dropped
her beer on the ground, slumping
into a heap. Dan took another long
sip before whistling loudly, signal-
ing two others who emerged from the
tree line.

"Well what do you know," Hodge
said quietly, "Looks like you were
right."

"It's almost like I can see
into the future or something,"
Artemis teased.

He side-glanced her. "We aren't
quite there yet."

"Yeah but we are getting closer." She held out her hands. "Why
don't you go ahead and un-cuff me
and I'll go rescue her?"

He blinked at her. "Why? I can
handle them."

"Because you are starting to
think I'm telling the truth. And be-

sides, after seeing what I did to Hauser, you really want to see what I can do in a fight." She smirked.

He stared at her for a moment, and then shrugged. "Eh what the hell, you have a point. Okay, give me your hands." He slid the key into the lock, freeing her.

She stretched her arms out wide and cracked her neck. "Okay, that's better. You wait here, I'm going to do disarm them."

He grabbed her arm as she began to walk away. "Hold up," he said, and pulled a knife from his pocket. "You're going to need something to defend yourself with."

She pulled out what appeared to be a normal blue LED laser pointer and held it up. "Nah, it's all good. I got it covered," she replied and winked at him.

His brow furrowed as he watched her stride into the clearing.

Dan and his two friends hovered around the heavily sedated Anna like vultures about to feast on their prey. The three of them looked like they would be right at home at a college bar, with their tight fitting t-shirts exposing their well developed physique and their hair containing enough gel to fill a kiddie pool.

"I gotta go take a piss," Dan said, "then we're gonna show this bitch a good time."

"Haha, yeah we are!" one of the two exclaimed. They gave each other a high five like obnoxious frat boys after a beer pong win.

Artemis quietly approached the duo from behind after Dan was out of earshot. She stopped about ten feet away, standing with her arms resting behind her back. A moment passed before she let out a soft whistle to get their attention.

"Hey boys," she purred.

"Damn baby, how you doing?" One of them asked.

The other one licked his lips. "Yeah, you looking for a little fun?"

"Well you *could* say that." She put a delicate-looking hand on her hip. "I don't know if the two of you can handle me though."

"Don't worry sweetheart, we're more than enough man for you," the first one replied as they flexed their muscles.

"Well, you say that." She raised an eyebrow. "But aren't you just waiting in line for sloppy seconds on that poor passed out girl there?"

The would-be rapists stopped flexing and went into a more defensive stance.

Artemis sneered. "I mean seriously, do you have to knock a girl out just so she won't laugh at your tiny, tiny dicks?"

Her opponents fumed.

"Bitch, I'm gonna knock you the fuck out and then we're going to have our fun with you before slitting your throat," the second one spat.

She struggled to contain her laughter. "I'll tell you what Tiny Dick, if you succeed then you two can have your way with me. I mean

I'm not really concerned given that I wouldn't feel anything anyway."

"Get her!" The first one yelled, shoving his partner in her direction.

He ran full steam towards Artemis, who remained in her casual pose. He led with his right fist in an attempt to knock her out with a single blow. She countered the punch by stepping slightly to the left, throwing her right arm around the back of his head and using his momentum to drive his face directly into the ground. Despite being a considerable distance away, Hodge heard the guy's nose cracking against the ground.

Her opponent writhed on the ground in pain, but Artemis wasn't finished with him yet. She pulled out the laser pointer and jammed it against his arm. The device made a *ka-chunk* noise as she hit the button on the end.

Her other opponent went on the attack, moving with purpose towards her as she stood up. He tried to

land a couple of haymakers and drew
nothing but air as she dodged them
with ease.

"What's wrong bud, having some
performance issues?" She taunted.

He let out a primal scream and
put his full weight into the next
punch.

She fell back to avoid the blow
while kicking her leg straight out,
landing a direct shot on his knee
and sending him staggering back into
a kneeling position. She popped up
off the ground and leapt into the
air, landing on his collar bone with
her knees. She drove him into the
ground, bones crunching beneath her.

Artemis hopped up. "No wonder
you have to drug your women," she
said. He made a weak grab for her,
but she just jammed the laser pointer against his arm like she'd done
to his buddy.

With the two frat boys indis-
posed, the deadly woman took a few
steps towards Anna. Just as she got
close, Dan emerged from the woods.

"Alright boys, let's do this,"
he bellowed, and then stopped short
at the two bodies on the ground.
"What the fu-"

She cut him off by driving her
foot into the side of his knee, ren-
dering the leg useless. As he
shrieked and fell, she grabbed the
his shirt collar and drove the laser
pointer into the back of his skull.
Ka-chunk. Artemis walked in front of
Dan and looked him in the eyes before rearing back and bootfucking
him right in the face.

Hodge watched in amazement from
the edge of the campsite as she
strolled back over to him. The two
lackeys pulled themselves off the
ground and made their way over to
Dan.

"You alright?" Hodge inquired
as he pulled his gun from its hol-
ster.

She nodded and winked at him.
"Yeah, feels good to get a workout
in."

"Well maybe next time instead
of counting how many calories you're

burning you should try focusing on your task," he retorted.

She raised an eyebrow. "My task?"

Hodge motioned towards the trio and aimed his gun towards them. "Yeah, your task. You said you were going to disarm them and you obviously didn't."

Dan looked positively murderous as he pulled his gun, and the three of them turned in Artemis' direction.

"Oh yeah, my bad," she said, and flicked the the side of the laser pointer before clicking the top button twice.

The lackeys fell to their knees immediately, screaming in agony. The injection site on their arms began to glow a bright red, causing the surrounding flesh to begin to bubble up and melt off of them. The process rapidly expanded from the injection site, their screams deafening as blood blisters formed on their skin and exploded, revealing the muscle and bone beneath.

With each pop the life drained from their body, their cries turning to moans and becoming quieter. Dan watched in horror as his two friends collapsed onto the ground beside him, their arms reduced to blood covered bone. His hands shook violently as he gaped at them.

Hodge's jaw was on the ground. "What the fuck was that?"

"Well, I said I was going to disarm them," Artemis replied.

He scoffed and stared at her with wide eyes. "We… we really need to work on our communication skills."

"Well now you know that I'm a very direct person, and I mean what I say," she declared.

He rolled his eyes. "Yeah, no shit!"

"I'm going to kill you motherfuckers!" Dan shrieked. "I'm going to kill both of you right here, then I'm going to find your families and-"

Artemis flicked another button on the side and gave the laser pointer one more click.

He immediately stopped talking as his eyes bugged out and started to bleed. He managed to squeal before his head exploded like it took a twelve-gauge shell at point blank range. His headless corpse crumpled to the ground.

"Ah, that's better," Artemis said as she stretched her arms above her head. "Wow, you can even hear the birds singing."

Hodge slowly holstered his weapon, still in a bit of shock. "Don't you think that was a little extreme?"

She glared at him. "They were going to rape and murder an unconscious woman then do it several more times, so no, I don't think that was too extreme."

"Point taken," he conceded. "So, how do we clean up this mess?"

She shook her head. "We don't."

"What do you mean we *don't*? There are three dead guys in the middle of the woods. I'm pretty sure there's going to be an investigation."

"I have no doubt, but it isn't going to go anywhere. The technology doesn't exist to trace my weapon, so we are in the clear," she explained, waving her magical death dealing laser pointer in the air.

He motioned to it. "Speaking of that, where in the hell did you get a laser pointer that melts limbs and explodes heads?"

"Oh, this? It came in the last shipment." She shrugged and pocketed her weapon.

He raised an eyebrow. "Shipment? Has the *Sharper Image* gone hardcore?"

"It's from my annual shipment from the future," she replied.

"Future shipment? So your friends in the future are sending you murderous cat toys? What else do they send you?"

"You can see for yourself if you like. The next shipment is due in about eight hours."

"Wow, that's convenient." He rolled his eyes.

"Robert and I discussed it, and we thought that if saving Anna from certain death wasn't enough to convince you that I was telling the truth, then seeing a crate of future technology appearing before your eyes would do it."

"Well let's just say I'm starting to believe, but if you can David Copperfield some future tech that should win me over." He sighed. "So where do we need to go?"

She motioned vaguely as she began to walk. "There is a warehouse about an hour outside of Austin. But we need to go ahead and take off because we need to stop by the office first."

"Woah woah, wait a second. What about Anna?" He put his hands up.

Artemis paused. "What about her?"

"We can't just leave her here," Hodge stammered. "Won't waking up to this mess traumatize her?"

"Maybe. At the very least she'll probably swear off internet dating." She shrugged. "I'll tell you what, if she isn't fine we'll come back."

"How the hell are we going to know that?" He threw his hands up.

She grinned. "Let's go to the office and I'll show you."

CHAPTER SIX

The door to the office cracked open, bathing the cluttered room in light. Artemis flipped on the overhead fluorescents.

"Woah!" Hodge exclaimed.

She chuckled. "Yeah, I know. It makes me look like I'm some sort of conspiracy theorist, doesn't it?"

"Just a bit, but I like it. Reminds me of my first office when I started this job," he replied as he studied her whiteboards.

She grabbed a marker, drawing a line through Dan's name and adding a seven to the *Saved* board.

Hodge leaned in for a closer look. "So what are these boards?"

"Well the top one is my most wanted list, and as you can tell I've made some progress," she explained. "The other board is the number of people I've saved."

"Wow, over sixteen thousand people saved? That's quite an impressive number. How many people have you had to kill to reach that?" he asked.

She shrugged. "I imagine it is pretty high, but I stopped counting when I got to five hundred."

"Oh yeah, when was that?" He cocked a brow.

"1972."

He gaped at her. Not just because of how prolific she had been over the years, but how she hadn't shown up on anyone's radar.

She booted up her laptop, drawing an amused look from the Agent.

"Wow, and I thought I was behind the times. Looks like that was cutting edge back in 2002," he teased.

She spun her office chair around and shot him a disapproving look. "Didn't your mother ever teach you that it's what is on the inside that counts?"

"No, she figured she had done enough for me by getting me named something other than Francis," he shot back.

Artemis nodded. "I tend to agree with her on that actually."

"So why are you using such an ancient piece of technology? I was expecting holograms and other fancy stuff." He ran a hand along a dusty filing cabinet.

She leaned back in her chair. "Only the case is ancient, most of the inner components won't be invented for another decade or two."

Hodge pursed his lips. "Okay, I still don't understand."

"Well, if you had a machine that could see into the future, would you want it to be nice and shiny Or would you want it to look like a worthless piece of junk?"

"That makes sense, just hide it in plain sight. I mean if I were a thief I wouldn't give that thing a second look," he agreed."

She smirked. "Now you're catching on."

"So how does that thing work exactly?" he asked, leaning in for a closer look.

She cocked her head. "Well, I can give you a lot of technical mumbo jumbo."

He rubbed his temple absently. "Please don't."

"For lack of a better term, this computer has a direct link to a computer in the future," she explained.

He put up a hand. "Wait, I thought you said the probe thingy only activated every five years or so."

"It does, but it constantly generates a small temporal rift. So while it isn't anywhere near large enough to send a person through, it's plenty big for small bits of data," she said.

His eyes widened. "So you can get news articles and stuff like that?"

"Exactly!" She smacked him triumphantly on the arm. "When they *do* send the shipment they include hard drives that has a snapshot of the internet. Every photo, website, video, et cetera, all in one tidy package."

He nodded thoughtfully. "But wait, doesn't that get out of date pretty quickly? Given how you are out there changing the future by taking our killers and all."

"On an individual level it can get out of date almost immediately," she agreed. "However, if you are trying to stop a terrorist attack it helps a great deal to have multiple documentaries breaking down every single thing that happened."

"Talk about having the tactical advantage," he mused.

She nodded. "You ain't kidding."

"So why can't you look up Duke on that thing?"

"All I have on him at the moment is out of date information from the last shipment. His timeline diverted off course about six months ago." She sighed.

Hodge leaned on her desk. "What do you mean?"

"Well, I was tracking him, and comparing his actions to what was on the shipment drive and they synced up perfectly," Artemis began.

"So why didn't you get him? Shouldn't he have been a priority?"

"He was on my list and I was working my way towards him." She sighed. "I finally had an opportunity to nab him six months ago, but he didn't show up to take out his intended victim."

"Who did he kill instead?"

She pointed to the President's board. "Number 49."

"Uh oh, they have their own board. Do I want to know who they were?" He leaned forward and squinted at the names.

"Those are, or were, the future presidents of this country."

His knees buckled a bit, forcing him to sit back on the edge of the desk. "Duke is killing future presidents? Why? No, wait, the better question is how?"

Artemis pointed at him as if to say *bingo*. "The only theory I have at the moment is that one of my former team members is trying to change the future and is using Duke as the muscle."

"Even if that is the case, shouldn't he still show up on your crystal ball computer there? I thought you got constant updates?" Hodge asked.

"Well," she replied, pausing for dramatic effect, "it's complicated."

He sighed. "Well, I wouldn't expect anything less from you at this point. Okay, explain it to me."

"If he is working closely with someone from my team then there is a good chance his future is tethered to theirs and hidden from me."

"Why do I get the sense I'm going to need ibuprofen for this?" Hodge moaned.

Without missing a beat, she reached to the far side of her desk and tossed him a pill bottle. He caught it and raised it in a mock toast.

"As I told you back at the bar, we exist outside the timeline, which means we don't show up anywhere unless we specifically act," Artemis continued. "For example, if I did a search for my future self it would come up empty unless I did something massive."

"But don't you do massive things every day? I mean you just killed three guys."

"There are seven and a half billion people on the planet. Three people isn't even a rounding error," she said. "Okay, think of it like this. Picture time like a raging river flowing free. What I did today was like throwing a pebble into it, just a small splash that is immediately forgotten. In order to show up I would have to drop a Raiders sized boulder into it."

"So what would qualify as a Raiders sized boulder?" He wrinkled his nose.

She spun around in her office chair. "Oh you know, the usual. Blowing up a city, releasing a plague that wipes out half the planet, winning a televised singing contest and becoming known the world over."

"So if Duke is doing the bidding and under the direction of someone like you, he would vanish from your future machine?"

"Exactly, which is why I need your help." She stopped spinning and tapped a few keys on the laptop. "You've been tracking him for years, so you might have insights that I wouldn't. It's one thing to read some articles online, it's another thing to eat sleep and breathe this case."

"You'd be right, but it's still a tough hill to climb and not at all depressing to think about. A mass murderer who can see the future? Holy fuck." He swallowed hard. "So... do you have any good news?"

She leaned back so he could see the screen. "Okay, here you go, some good news. The future of Anna Page."

Hodge leaned over her shoulder and saw an obituary from 2070. It was a lengthy piece documenting the life and times of Anna.

"Huh, look at that," he gushed. "Anna Page, ninety-one. Survived by her husband, four children, seven grandchildren and three great-grandchildren. Wow, so fourteen people will come into existence because of what we did today?"

"Yep. It's success stories like this that help me get past the knowledge that I destroy just as many lives simply by existing," Artemis replied.

He furrowed his brow, leaning back against the desk again. "What do you mean? How do you destroy lives? I mean besides the ones you explode."

"I don't belong in this time line, so something as simple as getting a cup of coffee or going to the movies can alter the future and wipe people from existence."

"Oh come on," he retorted, "don't get overdramatic on me now."

"It's true," she insisted. "How many times have you heard someone say that their big break in life was because they were in the right place at the right time? Hell, just look at your own life."

He blinked at her. "What about my life?"

"Think about when you met your wife," she continued. "You were both in Dallas at a conference and staying at the same hotel. You woke up early your last day there, went down to the lobby, got a cup of coffee, then made your way to the taxis. You and your future wife grabbed the door handle at the same moment. You both laughed before sharing the cab. Your stop was first, some greasy spoon breakfast joint you saw on one of the food channels. The two of you had such a great time chatting in the cab she joined you for breakfast. Before parting ways you exchanged numbers and made dinner plans for when you were both back in town. Since fate was on your side and you both lived in Austin. A year later you were engaged and expecting the first of your two children."

Hodge was stunned into silence
at the wealth of personal information Artemis had on him. It was one
thing to know about Francis, but
this was something else.

"Holy hell, did you get all of
that from your future telling machine there?"

She rolled her eyes. "No, you
just over shared during your an-
niversary post on social media.
You're in law enforcement. You
should have that shit on lockdown."

"Oh," he grunted, struggling to
find anything more than a single
syllable to express his embarrass-
ment.

"Now, imagine if I were staying
at that hotel and I got my coffee
the same time you did," she said.
"Instead of three people in front of
you there would be four. It's not
something you would notice or particularly care about, but it would
delay your schedule by about two
minutes."

Hodge's mind reeled at the
thought.

"If you get to the taxis two minutes later, you don't meet your wife," she continued. "Without that meeting your two children aren't born. Your future grandkids are never born. When you and your wife marry other people, the children that would have resulted from your partners other relationships are never born. Even if we stop there that's what? Ten, twelve people who are wiped from existence. All because I got coffee in the morning."

He put his hands up. "Yeah, but other lives take their place. It's not like you are willingly taking innocent lives out."

"I know. But it doesn't matter." She took a deep breath. "Using this computer I can look up anyone and see the entirety of their lives. They exist, right now. They may not have been born yet but I can see everything. They have family, friends, coworkers. Some of them do extraordinary things. About forty years ago I saw a documentary about Josie Chambers, and in 2014 she became the youngest woman to win a Nobel prize in Physics. She made some breakthrough that was far too technical even for me to fully grasp, but it revolutionized the field and she was heralded as one of the brightest minds of her time." She pursed her lips, gaze downcast.

Hodge crossed his arms. "So what happened?"

"I was on the job in Chicago, and it was a rough one," she replied, fiddling with the hem of her shirt. "There was a serial killer that was targeting nurses when they got off their shift, and by the end of his reign he claimed eighteen lives. I got to the scene late and he had a woman sliced open. I saw him there covered in her blood, grinning like a madman and it sent me into a rage. Normally I kill using technology so I don't risk detection, but I beat this guy with my bare hands. Beat him so badly that he was unrecognizable. Needless to say I needed to cool off, so after getting cleaned up I hit the hotel bar.

"About four drinks in a young man bought me a drink and we got to chatting. Nothing sleazy happened mind you, but we ended up talking till closing. We parted ways and I went back to my room to pass out. About a week later when I was back home I decided to look up Josie to see what else she did, and I couldn't find anything. Turned out that the man I was having drinks with that night was friends with her future mother. He got into an acci-dent on the drive home and ended up in the hospital for several weeks. He didn't have any family in the area, so Josie's future mom took care of him, and in the process fell for him instead of Josie's future father. So because I had a drink with someone, one of the brightest minds in the history of the world ceased to exist. Knowledge like that can wear on you."

"I… I can't imagine." He shook his head at her slowly. "That must be really difficult for you, and well, your entire team."

"I think I'm the last one who cares actually." She shrugged. "Once we put the country on the right path, most of the surviving team retired. They just wanted to get out of history's way as best they could and enjoy the new future we had created. In fact the only other active meddler I know is Brent."

"Does he hunt bad guys like you?"

She chuckled. "No. Actors."

"Actors? Why in the world would he do that?" He leaned on his hands again.

"Well he's a big TV and movie guy," she explained. "Has an incredible home theater system, one hundred and twenty-five inch projection screen with surround sound. Even sprung for the professional 3D glasses. Whenever I'm done copying over the information I need from the shipment I send him the drive with all the entertainment."

"You send him future Netflix?" Hodge asked.

"Something like that. An entire century's worth of movies and TV shows. Every now and then an actor will get cast in a role he loves and they ruin it. When that happens Brent will intervene so a better actor gets the role."

He gasped. "My god that's terrible! He kills people if he doesn't like their acting?"

"No, no." She waved her hands in front of her face, but then froze. "Well. Okay, rarely. Usually he just sabotages their career or does something that keeps them from a role."

"Like what?"

"So Brent is a huge Marvel fan, especially the X-men and Wolverine in particular." She rolled her eyes, a ghost of a smile on her lips at the memory. "For *years* he ranted about how they miscast Wolverine with Dougray Scott and wanted to get him out of the role. He enjoyed his work and didn't want to destroy his career, so he devised a plan. Brent went to where they were shooting Mission Impossible 2, which was his project before joining the X-men, and he caused all sorts of problems and delays with the production. Nothing major, just convincing a few key people to leave the shoot, as well as a few other minor shenani-gans. The shoot went over schedule, Scott had to drop out, Hugh Jackman become one of the largest stars in the world, and I never had to hear Brent complain about how the role was miscast again."

Hodge ran a shaky hand through his hair. "Wow that's a hell of a story. I don't think it's right, but still, you have to admire the dedi-cation."

"After what he went through in the war I figure he's earned the right," she said quietly.

"What did he go through in the war?"

"It's a long story, but the nickel version is that we were in Germany and he's Jewish," she explained. "It took us weeks to track him down and we lost a couple of team members liberating him. Between the experience and the guilt of his friends losing their life because of him he just shut down."

"That's harsh. You're right, he's earned the right," he agreed, trying to keep his tone light. "Just try to keep his murdering to a minimum, unless the actor is *really* terrible."

Artemis chuckled and noticed the clock on the wall. "We need to get going. It's a bit of a drive to the warehouse to get the shipment, and it's almost time."

He nodded. "Alright, let's do it."

CHAPTER SEVEN

Hodge was restless as they ventured far outside the city. He was not a fan of long car trips, and certainly not a fan of being on unpaved country roads. Twenty minutes of jostling around due to the dirt road took its toll.

"You know, if you wanted to kill me and dump my body you could have just left me with Dan and his crew instead of going through the trouble of dragging me all the way out here," he joked.

Artemis grinned at her passenger. "Aw, are you getting scared Hodge? You not a fan of being in the middle of nowhere?"

"I've seen enough horror films to know this is the beginning of one. Pretty sure a guy in a human skin mask and a chainsaw is going to pop out at any minute," he replied.

She laughed. "Don't worry, we are out this far because of safety concerns. We were fortunate that the time machine delivers people and packages into the middle of nowhere. Made it a lot easier to buy the land way back when."

"So do you have any backup coming in case Duke and his puppet master show up?"

"Unfortunately it's just the two of us. Outside of you the only other person I trust is Robert, and he's not a fighter."

"Not a fighter?" Hodge asked. "What, he didn't help you out during the war?"

"When we arrived, we discussed tracking him down, because we needed all the help we could get with the war effort. Ultimately we decided against it because at that time we had no idea if that would disrupt the timeline," she explained.

He furrowed his brow. "What do you mean?"

"We were afraid that if we contacted him before he made *Day of the Demon* it would create a paradox. If we pulled him into the war and he died, he wouldn't be in the movie, I never would have saw it and known that the time machine was actually a time machine."

Hodge nodded. "Okay, that makes sense."

"It wasn't until the fifties that we discovered we were outside the timeline," she said.

"How did you discover that exactly? It doesn't sound like a theory you would want to test out on yourself."

"Yeah nobody was really lining up to be the guinea pig on that one," she agreed. "After the war, there were a small handful of us still active, working as a team to ensure that the future we had created remained intact. I was the main researcher and had numerous search protocols set up to look for any of our ancestors. With what we did in Europe, we had altered the timeline in a massive way. We saved tens of millions of lives and not all of them were good ones, you know?"

He nodded. "So in addition to saving Suzy Homemaker you also saved Ted Bundy wannabes."

"Exactly," she said as she dodged a pothole on the gravel road. "So when the shipment came through in 1949, I ran a search on all of our ancestors to make sure everyone was alive and well."

"And I'm guessing someone wasn't?" he mused.

"Well, yes and no. Everyone's great-grandparents were alive, but not hooking up with who they originally did."

"I can see that," he said. "I mean, the war uprooted millions of people in this country, especially compared to what you have told me about the war in your time. Not just soldiers being shipped overseas, but people having different careers, interacting with different people. It's like your coffee example only on steroids."

"Exactly. Once we discovered this I did an extensive search through everyone's family tree. Out of the five of us in the group, only one of us had a record of being born."

"And since none of you did the Marty McFly vanishing act, that was a pretty clear indication that you were outside the timeline," he concluded.

She nodded. "That's true, but it didn't really sink in for us until we met up for the 1965 shipment. In the late forties we went our separate ways, taking up residence in separate parts of the country. A couple of us kept hunting down the bad guys, but for the most part everyone was retired and lived their own lives. When everyone walked into the room it was hard not to notice the fact nobody had aged a day since over the past four decades. We kind of put two-and-two together at that point."

"Well as far as problems go, I guess that's a good one to have. I've had more than my fair share of run-ins with people who have gone to great lengths to retain the appearance of youth." Hodge smiled.

Artemis chuckled. "I know, I read up on your stripper murder investigation."

"Terrible case, but totally didn't mind doing the witness interviews," he admitted.

She scoffed. "I'm sure your wife would be thrilled to hear that."

"Hey now, just because you've ordered doesn't mean you can't look at the menu," he replied, and then his face went pale. "Please don't tell my wife I said that."

"You're lucky I like you Hodge," she said as she slowed down. "We're here."

He gazed upon the fortress-like structure that stood in the middle of a clearing. Double twenty foot tall barbed wire fences, reinforced concrete walls, and no apparent door made this an imposing building. If anybody stumbled across this on a hike they would most certainly turn and walk the other way.

"Holy hell, that's a building," he murmured.

She shrugged. "Well we had the resources so we decided to make this place as secure and imposing as possible to make sure nobody would intercept our supplies if we happened to be late to a drop."

"I'm pretty sure you succeeded in that. I mean I don't even see a door."

Artemis winked and punched a lengthy code into her cell phone. After completion the barbed wire fences opened up and part of the grey concrete on the building bubbled away to reveal a giant steel door.

Hodge's eyes widened. "When we survive this and catch Duke, can I put in an order with you for some future tech?" he asked.

"Sure, you'll just have to wait five years to get it." She shrugged.

"Wait, seriously?" He furrowed his brow as he followed her inside. "How do you put in orders? Can you communicate with the future?"

"In a manner of speaking. Before we left we created a messaging system using books," she replied.

He raised an eyebrow. "Books?"

"Yeah, we knew we'd have money and could get anything published we wanted," Artemis explained, "so we each have a pen name to write under. In the beginning we bought our way into dime store sci-fi novels and magazines. We would include what we needed as items in the story as a plot device, like explosive ammo or an extra laptop. When it came time for the shipment to be assembled by our team in the future, they would search for pen names, read the stories and fulfill the orders.

"We had to get a little creative with the names once we figured out we were borderline immortal, so we passed the legacy on to our children. Technically I'm a third generation sci-fi writer with a rather impressive online following." She grinned and puffed her chest out a little bit.

"Wait, what's your pen name? I read a lot of sci-fi growing up," he gushed like a schoolgirl at a boy band concert.

She laughed. "What? No, I'm not telling."

"Aww come on I really want to know if I'm your fanboy." He pouted.

"It's my secret. Superman doesn't go around telling people he's Clark Kent, after all."

"Wait, so you'll openly share with me your a time traveling warrior who has killed an untold number of people, but you won't tell me your pen name?"

She simply shrugged.

"Okay." He sighed.

"I'll tell you what, you help me kill Duke and catch my former team member, and I'll give you a hint." Her eyes twinkled.

"Deal," he replied with a thumbs up. "So how long until the shipment arrives?"

She checked her phone. "About fifteen minutes."

CHAPTER EIGHT

The duo walked around the cavernous building, kicking up dust as they went along. Artemis had been the only visitor here for decades and cleanliness hadn't been very high up on her list. The bulk of the floor plan consisted of an empty space, lined with rooms against the far wall with heavily tinted windows.

"Welcome to the warehouse, home of the amazing time-traveling shipments." She spread her arms for dramatic effect.

"So now what?" Hodge asked, voice echoing.

She led him into one of the small rooms. "We hang out here, look away from the windows, and drink them if you got them."

He pulled a flask from his pocket and toasted her with it. "Cheers!"

"I knew there was a reason I picked you as a partner," she said as they took a seat on the floor.

He leaned back on his hand as he offered her the flask. "So how do we know when the shipment arrives? Does it do that giant electrical storm thing from the Terminator? Oh god, nobody is going to be naked are they?"

"No on both fronts there," she replied and then took a sip. "Since we don't age, there is no need to send back more people, and we'll know when the shipment arrives when this room is bathed in light."

"Even through the blacked out windows?" Hodge asked as he looked up towards them.

Artemis quickly shielded his eyes and pulled his view back to the ground. "Yes, even through the windows. Trust me, you don't want to be looking that direction when it comes in, unless of course you want to be blinded in a horrific manner."

"I would think any sort of blinding would be horrific." He laughed.

She deadpanned. "Well, there is losing your eyesight and there is having your eyeballs melt."

"Man you future people don't fuck around do you? Exploding limbs, melting eyeballs. I mean, is there anything in the future that isn't nightmare inducing?"

"Nope, it's pretty much a non-stop orgy of chaos and mayhem."

"Damn, it's a shame I won't live long enough to see it." Hodge shook his head.

Before the conversation could continue, the room illuminated. Even with the protective windows, Hodge and Artemis had to shield their eyes from the light. After about thirty seconds everything returned to normal.

"Alright, let's go get our future care package," she said and hopped to her feet.

The two of them walked out into the center of the room towards three large plastic tubs sitting on the floor. A bit of residual smoke hovered about, looking like a discount magician didn't purchase enough dry ice for his show.

He crossed his arms. "Wow, I was expecting something a little more futuristic."

"What?" She shrugged. "They are cheap and effective. Plus we have to do everything we can to remain hidden, so a shiny futuristic box isn't a great thing to have laying around."

"Plus there was a spare room filled with these things back at the bunker," a man's voice boomed behind them.

Artemis whipped around in a defensive stance and Hodge drew his gun. Both of them remained on guard as six foot four blonde haired perfect specimen of a man emerged from the shadows. His physique made him look as though he was carved out of granite, and when combined with his height made him an imposing foe.

Artemis squinted, and then her arms relaxed. "Rudo? Is that you?" she asked with a sense of disbelief. "My god, I thought you were dead.

Nobody has heard from you in damn near forty years."

Rudo paused about ten feet away from the duo, giving the Agent a sense of uneasiness. "Well, I have had some troubles in recent years that forced me underground. All because I dared to live a normal life for a while in this new future we created."

"What, did you get a wife, two and a half kids and a house with a white picket fence?" she retorted.

"All of that actually," he admitted. "Back in sixty-seven I met this wonderful woman named Mary. She worked as a waitress at this small town diner just outside of Nashville, and I fell hard for her. After what we went through in the war and all those years tracking down the worst of the worst, I just wanted a chance to be a normal person, even if it was just for a little bit." He smiled. "Took me a while to win her over, but once I did, we hit the road and left everything behind. Spent two years traveling the world.

It was so amazing to see the world through her eyes, and frankly nice to see Europe again without having to worry about Nazi death squads around every corner.

"By seventy-two we had settled back in Nashville, married with two kids, Bill and Sasha. Had the biggest house on the block and enough in the bank to pay someone to mow the lawn because let's be real, I'll gladly track a serial killer across four states, but I'll be damned if I'm going to mow a lawn as big as Volunteer stadium. I had it all, but by the late nineties a problem arose."

"Let me guess, everyone got older but you?" Hodge cut in.

"You are quite correct, Special Agent Hodge. At first I was able to pass it off as good genes, but that only worked for so long," Rudo replied.

The Agent paled. "Wait, how do you know my name?"

"Patience, Agent Hodge, patience." The tall man sneered. "May
I continue?"

"Oh, I'm sorry, by all means."

"Mary began to question why I
still looked the same as I did when
we met thirty some odd years ago.
After a lot of consideration I made
the decision to trust the woman I
had dedicated a large portion of my
life to and told her the truth."

Artemis winced. "Oh, Rudo."

"I know. Believe me I know," he
said, putting up his hands. "I sat
her down and told her everything.
Even showed her the computer and let
her get a glimpse of the future. I
thought that coming clean would make
everything okay. Instead of feeling
relieved however, she felt betrayed
that I had been lying to her since
the moment we met. Over the next few
weeks our relationship fell apart.
At first it was non-stop arguments,
then it was on to the silent treat-
ment. I was hoping she just needed
time to adjust, but ultimately that
was a foolish hope.

"One morning she asked if I would go to the store for her. At first I thought this was her finally coming around, but I didn't trust it, even though I desperately wanted to. I drove around the neighborhood park a couple of times and did a drive-by of the house before running the errand. There was a black SUV in the driveway. My heart sank because I knew exactly who they were. I went into my house and found her at the kitchen table with two agents and my computer. I… I'll spare you the details of what happened next, but let's just say that there is a lengthy disclaimer that is attached to any real estate listing of that property."

"My god Rudo," Artemis breathed. "Did you kill your wife? Your kids?"

"I didn't have a choice," he moaned, eyes shining with tears. "I had to eliminate anyone I had been close to in order to protect the secret."

Hodge clenched his fists. "Bullshit!"

"It's not bullshit," Rudo snapped. "She has undoubtedly shown them the computer. Can you imagine what our government—hell, *any* government would do with that technology? It had to be protected at all costs, even the price I paid." He paused. "After I committed those atrocities I had to fake my own death so there wouldn't be a manhunt. Luckily I was able to get ahead of it and nobody outside of the deceased knew of what I possessed.

"Still, even though I know I did what had to be done, my actions took a severe toll on me. And to make matters worse most of the tech was damaged beyond repair in the process, leaving me with a limited knowledge base."

Artemis shook her head, disgust evident on her face. "Christ, how many people had to die because you wanted to have a normal life?"

"Only about half a dozen," he replied. "And really, who are *you* to pass judgement on *me*, standing beside Agent Hodge here."

She clenched her jaw. "This is different."

"You're right, you only have to kill one person instead of six."

Hodge glanced at her. "Wait, you are planning on killing me?"

"Only if you get chatty," she shot back.

He shrugged. "Eh, fair enough."

Rudo chuckled. "Oh Artemis, it is so good to see you again after all these years. It warms my heart to know that even after a century on this earth you are still as confident and cocky as always."

"And you are still as cold and ruthless as you were back in the war," she replied. "But those were different times, and we didn't kill anyone we didn't absolutely have to."

"Well, in my view everyone I've killed has been out of necessity."

He raised his chin. "Just like forty-eight through sixty."

She stiffened. "So you *are* Duke's handler."

"I don't know if handler is the correct word," Rudo replied, and tapped his chin in mock thought. "Duke, what do you think?"

"I'm kind of partial to mentor actually." Duke emerged from the darkness with two henchmen, guns drawn and trained on the duo.

Anthony Duke was a compact powerhouse of a human being. He was only 5'4, but thanks to a combination of a six days a week workout regiment and a healthy dose of anabolic steroids, he was nearly as wide as he was tall. While his two henchmen Pete and Rocco towered over him, Duke had the core strength to lift them both off their feet simultaneously.

The lackeys both looked like they would be right at home in a dive bar throwing back whatever cheap beer was on special that night. The only thing that set the two of them apart was a large scar on the left side of Rocco's face.

"Which one do you want me to kill first?" Duke asked while moving the barrel of his gun back and forth between the two.

"Neither," Rudo snapped. "Artemis and I have been through more together than you can comprehend, and I'm not going to be the reason she dies if I can help it."

His pawn pouted. "So what should we do with them?"

"See if our friend Agent Hodge has some handcuffs on him and secure them," Rudo instructed. "Please make sure they are comfortable, as they will be here for a while."

Duke nodded in acknowledgment before moving towards the duo. "Okay you two, move over to the steel beams near the wall and get comfy. My two friends Pete and Rocco will handcuff you."

"Once you have them secure, start loading up the truck," Rudo said. He walked over to Artemis, now secured to the beam, and knelt beside her. "I hate that it's come to this, Artemis. We have been through so much together. We rampaged through Europe together while taking down one of the most fearsome empires the world has ever seen.

"You and I, we prevented billions from perishing. We created a world far superior than even our wildest dreams could come up with." He brushed a lock of her hair back from her face. "You know, it could even be argued that you and I are two of the most important people ever to exist in the history of the world. We have done more to shape the path of humanity than anybody who isn't currently worshiped by billions."

"Then why are you doing this?" she asked. "Why are you being a mentor to a psychopath and murdering the future leaders of our country?"

"I lost the ones I loved because I had to protect our secret from governments that would misuse it," he replied. "However, if *I* were in charge and the entire world knew

I was an immortal who could see into the future, there wouldn't be a secret to protect now would there?"

Her jaw fell open. "So you are going on a killing spree just so you can be President?"

"President, omnipotent god king, I'm open to whatever title they bestow upon me." He grinned.

She scowled. "You're crazy if you think the general public is going to elect an egotistical narcissist like you."

"They will when I'm the only viable option. Now that I have updated equipment I can see the future in real time again. It's just a matter of taking out my opponents until I get one I can win against, either by their incompetence or by being able to dig up dirt on them for that October surprise that hits every election. And the beauty of having an apprentice like Duke is I don't even have to do the heavy lifting."

"You do know I'm going to do everything in my power to stop you, right?" She jutted out her chin.

"Frankly, I would be disappointed if you didn't," Rudo replied. "In reality I should just kill you and your partner now, but I have faith in you Artemis. I know that more than anything you want America to be the greatest it can possibly be. With me in charge, knowing all the things I will know, it *will* be the greatest."

"We set out on a mission to save the country from destruction, not rule over it," she hissed.

"But if I rule it, we save it not only for today but for all eternity. I think once you see that you'll understand that I'm right. And when that day comes I hope that you'll join me." He pointed to the case still in the center of the room. "You see that? I'm leaving you a case of gear so you can see just how successful I am in this venture. I assume you are still sending movies out to Brent?"

She nodded, jaw clenched tight.

"Now, one of my associates will be dropping by here in 24 hours to give you a key for these handcuffs. Don't bother interrogating him because he won't know where I'll be. When you get back home with the equipment, look up the bright future I will provide for our country. Then continue what you have been doing all these years. Saving the little guy."

"I swear to god Rudo, I'm going to stop you!" she snarled.

"I admire your optimism. However by the time you are released from these cuffs I'll be far away from here. And we both know that thanks to our unique relationship with time I will be completely insulated from your reach until I'm in a position of power." He stood up and began to walk away before turning around. "I sincerely hope that once you've had a chance to look at the future you'll decide to join me. Although if this is indeed the final time we are face to face, I just want you to know how appreciative I am of all the sacrifices you've made over the years in making our nation stronger.

And for the record, by leaving you
and your friend alive I'm consider-
ing my debt to you paid in full.
Good luck Artemis."

Rudo and his gang left the
warehouse, slamming the door behind
them and leaving the prisoners in
relative darkness. The two of them
sat in silence for a few moments before Hodge broke it.

"Any idea what time it is?" he
asked.

Artemis chuckled. "Why, you
have somewhere to be?"

"Well he said in 24 hours he is
going to be gone, so I just wanted
to know what our deadline is," he
said.

"Well my arms are behind my
back, so I can't see my watch, but
if I had to guess I'd say about one
in the morning. Not that it matters
much, seeing as how we are stuck
here."

"What, you don't have a fancy
gadget that can get us out of these
cuffs? What about your laser pointer
of death?"

"Yeah, that would work perfectly, if it wasn't in my front
pocket."

"Well damn." He sighed, and
fidgeted in the darkness. "So what
did he mean by his debt being paid
in full?"

"It's kind of a long story,"
she muttered.

He chuckled. "Well, as fate
would have it, I have some time to
kill."

"This is true," she replied.
"During the war, a mission Rudo was
heading up went south and he ended
up getting captured, giving himself
up so that the other members of the
team, including myself, could es-
cape. Our commander made the decision to cut our losses and focus on
the main task. I disagreed with his
order and went on a solo rescue mission."

"Goddamn you are one hardcore
woman," he blurted.

"Oh you have no idea." She
laughed. "He was being held at this
small POW work camp close to the

border with Poland with about a hundred other men. The Germans had them working in a factory producing something or other. I'm not sure what they were making there, but whatever it was it warranted a heavy guard presence which made my job all the more difficult. I spent a day doing recon and had planned on doing a few more, but my timeline was moved up when I witnessed them execute a prisoner in the courtyard. I went in that night."

"How did you take out an entire work camp on your own?" He asked while continuing to move about.

"Luckily it was a moonless night, so I was able to slip in undetected and into one of the bunkhouses," she explained. "Rudo wasn't in the first one, but a dozen angry Polish men were. We didn't speak the same language, however when I pulled out a fist full of knives and tossed it onto the bed I'd like to believe we connected. They armed themselves and after some crude hand gesturing and pointing at blonde hair they understood who I was looking for. One of them had me follow him to the appropriate building while the others began taking out the guards one by one.

"About thirty seconds after I reached Rudo, gunshots began to ring out. We didn't know if it was the guards retaking control or if our Polish friends had upgraded their weapons. We didn't stick around long enough to find out. We spent the next five weeks on the run, evading capture and raising as much hell as we could. Unfortunately in the process we endangered the main mission, but that's another story for another time."

"Well that explains why you two didn't want to kill each other. Kind of hard to go through something like that together and not be close," he said as he continued to fidget.

"Yeah, we've been through some shit together. And..." Artemis paused and watched Hodge begin to really squirm about. "What in the hell are you doing?"

"In all your research on me, did you ever look really closely at my college years?" he asked.

She raised an eyebrow. "Well I know you went into Tech, got a degree in criminal psychology with a minor in classic lit. Not sure how that explains whatever you are doing at the moment."

"It can be difficult to make ends meet as a college student. Some of my classmates waited tables, a few of them stripped. And me?" He pulled his arms free and held up the pair of opened handcuffs. "I was a street magician."

Her jaw dropped. "You have got to be kidding me."

"Yeah, I'm just fucking with you." He chuckled as he made his way over to her. "I had a crazy as hell girlfriend in college who was into some really kinky stuff. One night she left me handcuffed to her roommate's bed and left to go to the bar. It was really awkward a couple of hours later when her roommate came home with his date only to find a naked man chained to his bed."

She barked a laugh. "That must have been a mood killer for him."

"Unfortunately, his boyfriend was a lot more open to the situation than I would have hoped," he said with a sigh as he unlatched her cuffs. "Ever since that incident I've had a handcuff key sewn into the sleeves of all my shirts."

"Just for the record, if we survive this and save the country from being taken over by a madman, we'll leave out the part where we were saved thanks to your paranoia brought on by kinky sexcapades gone wrong," she declared.

He nodded. "That's probably a good call."

"Come on, let's grab the gear and get back to the office."

Artemis burst through the office door and made a beeline for her computer, leaving Hodge to drag in the crate of gear. Once he finally got into the room and kicked the door shut, he ripped open the lid and began digging through the box.

"What am I looking for?" he asked.

She glanced over her shoulder. "It's going to look like a bright silver USB key. Should be near the top."

He rummaged some more and then found it, tossing it over to her. She plugged it into the side of her laptop and began typing away.

He leaned over her shoulder. "What are you searching for?"

"Anything about Rudo," she said. "If he is serious about running the country he's going to show up on this drive. Then all we have to do is work backwards to see when he first shows up and hope there is a way to get to him."

His brow furrowed. "I don't understand. He's had this plan for a while now, why couldn't you have found him before now? Don't you have a direct link to future news?"

"Well, for starters, I wasn't looking for him because I thought he was either retired or dead," she explained. "Secondly, even if I *was* looking for him it's highly unlikely I would have found anything since before today he didn't have the technology at his disposal to win. I mean I have a deep seeded plan to become the first female host of Family Feud, but I don't have the means to actually accomplish it, so I wouldn't show up if I searched for myself in the future, does that make sense?"

He nodded, and she took a deep breath as she continued to type.

"The moment he entered the warehouse and got in position to get the jump on us he solidified his future, and now that he has a constant link to the future news he has the means to achieve his goal. This will hopefully be a big enough splash to force him into the timeline." She leaned forward, lips pursed.

Hodge scratched the back of his head. "So how do you track him? Just type his name into future google?"

"Hardly," Artemis replied with a shake of her head. "He's going to have to come up with a fake identity in order to run for office. Partly because he isn't technically born for another decade or so, and partly because if he ran under his real name he'd have to explain why his family and a couple of government agents were found dead in his house. I'm gong to start looking ten years in the future. If he does become President I can get a name and work backwards from there, hopefully finding him at a low enough level where he isn't surrounded by a massive protection detail."

"Then what?"

"No clue. But first things first. We have to find him." She grunted as the search turned up *No Results Found*. "What the fuck?"

He bit his lip. "That can't be good."

"No, no it's not," she muttered. "I'm searching news sources ten years from now and can't find anything."

"Wait, why isn't that good news? If you can't find him then maybe he wasn't successful."

"You don't understand, I can't find anything about anybody. Every news source I use is simply *gone* ten years from now," she said.

Hodge's knees buckled a bit, sending him against the edge of the desk. Artemis continued to type, getting more frustrated as she went along.

"Jesus, nothing at nine years… eight… seven… okay here we go, finally," she said, and leaned forward to squint at the fine print. "Well, he's President six years from now."

He swallowed and cocked his head, still not trusting his legs. "Wow, from nobody to President in six years. Guess knowing everything has its advantages."

"No kidding."

"So what did he do? Why did everything vanish?" he asked, mouth dry.

She clicked the mouse a few times to move forward in the time-line. "My guess is that it has something to do with the fact that World War Three broke out."

"How the hell did that happen?" His eyes widened.

"A few months after being sworn into office, he went and addressed the United Nations. During the speech Rudo decided he wanted to let the world know he had the ability to see into the future," she said as she skimmed the articles.

He rolled his eyes. "I'm sure that went over well."

"Everybody thought it was a joke and that he had some sort of mental break. Nobody took him seriously and other world leaders, not to mention every light night comedy show host, mocked him mercilessly. They stopped laughing a week later when he exposed some third world dictatorship's program to develop WMDs."

"How did he manage that? He send in spies or something?" he asked.

"He was able to provide a photo of the country's leader standing in the WMD facility," she replied, pointing to the photo on the screen. "Took it from the country's grade school history book that was written fifty years from now. With that photographic evidence he was able to justify a preemptive invasion, and it was brutal. He micromanaged the entire war from the Situation Room, doling out orders on a near hourly basis to minimize casualties. Knowing every single battle and how it went down was an amazing tactical advantage for our troops. Took all of four days for the country to be pacified, with our death toll under a hundred. And in typical Rudo fashion, he put the rest of the world on notice that if they tried anything against the USA they would meet the same fate."

"And let me guess, the other nations didn't like the idea of a rogue US President having the ability to see into the future?" Hodge retorted.

"Yeah, not so much," Artemis agreed. "Within weeks of the demonstration, China, Russia, and Europe came together and demanded that Rudo share the technology with them so that they could prevent attacks on their soil, as well as keeping the USA in check. When he refused, the rest of the nations came together and deemed America the enemy of the world. The war was short and brutal, with America dominating all comers. Unfortunately for Rudo, and really everyone, Russia had a secret stockpile of nukes that was just far enough away from the US reach. They were able to get off a barrage of nuclear missiles before their country was overrun."

"I'm sure Rudo took that well."

"See for yourself," she said, and hit *play* on a video of President Rudo.

"My fellow Americans," he said, spreading his arms. "A few short months ago, you placed your trust in me to make America the greatest nation that has ever existed in the history of the world. We became so great that our supposed allies got jealous and wanted to take us down a notch or two so we would be at their level. At first they just wanted what we had, but when I, your President, refused to hand it over they made the decision to destroy it and us. As I deliver this message to you a barrage of nuclear weapons are bearing down on our great nation. Within the hour everything that we have build over the centuries, every bit of greatness will be vaporized. But fear not my people, for we will not go quietly into that good night. I have ordered the launching of every missile within our arsenal. With our dying breath as a nation we will strike back at our assaulters with such fury and force that it will crack the Earth itself. Even though we will no longer be here, you can rest in peace knowing that our actions and our greatness will remain forever. Godspeed, and God bless America!"

"There are also an alarming number of livestream videos of the world ending, which I'll spare us," Artemis muttered, and closed the program window.

The hair on the back of Hodge's neck stood straight up. "Holy hell, that was all kinds of terrifying. Didn't take long for all that power to go straight to his head."

"You have to understand, Rudo was always the most dedicated, most patriotic among our group," she said. "When we discovered we could go back and alter history, he was the first one to volunteer. During the years before we left he did tireless research on the war, learned multiple regional languages, and familiarized himself with every resistance group that we might come across. By the time we hit Europe he knew exactly what needed to be done in order to accomplish the mission.

He was, and is, willing to do whatever it takes to make our country the greatest."

"So even if we show him this video and the aftermath of nothingness he won't abandon his plans?"

"Unfortunately no. This will only get him to work harder and try to find a way to achieve his goals of American supremacy."

He sighed. "So how do we stop him?"

"I don't know yet. I need time to trace his steps," she said, leaning back in her seat. "Hodge, it's five in the morning. There is a comfy spot in the corner there if you want to get some rest. It's going to take me a while to figure out our next move."

He hesitated, but then nodded in his exhaustion. "Okay, but if you find anything, or if I can do anything at all, no matter how small, then you wake me up."

She smiled. "Just hit go on the coffee maker and I'll be good."

Hodge shot Artemis a thumbs up before making his way towards the makeshift bed. He crashed out to the sound of furious keystrokes.

CHAPTER TEN

The sun peeked through the drawn blinds at the office, reflecting gently off of Artemis' stained coffee mug. She was still typing away when Hodge awoke from his short nap.

"Ugh, what time is it," he asked, wandering over to her desk.

She glanced at the corner of her screen. "About nine."

"You had any luck tracking him down?" He ran a hand through his hair, yawning painfully.

"Not really," she replied. She picked up her coffee mug and waved it in Hodge's general direction as a signal for a refill. "The first sign of him I have is six weeks from now in Rhode Island when he gets a job as the Chief of Staff for a member of the US House."

"Great," he said, returning with an extra mug and the full pot of coffee. "Then we just have a road trip and get him in six weeks."

She shook her head. "By then it'll be too late. He'll be in the public eye, surrounded by security. Not to mention Duke and his henchmen."

"I'm guessing Duke didn't show up either?" he asked as he refilled her mug.

She inclined her head in thanks and took a sip. "Nope, they are both completely off the grid until six weeks from now."

He sat on his favorite corner of the desk and nursed his coffee for a beat before something clicked in his brain. "Wait, what about the henchmen? Can we track him through them?"

"It's unlikely, since Rudo doesn't keep people around him very long," she replied. "After a few days of work, he'll pay them off with a couple of hot sports betting tips so they can make a fortune. He also lets them know if they talk it won't be that difficult for him to track them down, so they obey and keep quiet about it."

He shrugged. "You have a better idea?"

She paused and then shook her head. "Nope, I don't. Okay, so what do we know about these two?"

"I heard Duke call them Pete and Rocco, and one of them had a facial scar," Hodge replied, running a finger down his cheek.

Artemis sighed. "It could take days to find a match, and we don't have that kind of time."

"Let me make a call," he said, and pulled out his phone. "I have a C.I. who owes me a few favors. If these guys have been active in the area he might be able to help out. Just a word of warning though, he's a bit salty."

"Don't worry, I'm R-Rated." She winked at him and then turned back to the computer.

Hodge dialed the phone and put it on speaker. It rang multiple times before a groggy voice on the other end finally answered.

"What?"

The Agent leaned over his phone. "Hey Jimbo, it's Hodge. Listen, I need a favor."

"Motherfucker it's nine in the goddamn morning. Don't you know people like me sleep in the daytime?" Jimbo barked.

"I'm sorry man, if I had any other options I would take them. I kind of got a life or death situation over here."

"Dude save me your sob story. Just get to the point so I can go back to bed. My bitches are getting cold."

Hodge nodded. "Alright, I'm looking for a guy I had a run-in with last night. Rough looking dude, has a nasty scar on his left cheek, goes by either Pete or Rocco."

"Quiet dude who looks like he's gotten his ass kicked a few too many times?"

"Yeah that sounds about right," the Agent replied.

"That sounds like Rocco Giovani, AKA Rocky G. Used to run some errands for me a while back till he fucked me over and I had to show him the door," Jimbo drawled.

"Thanks, Jimbo, you're awesome."

"Yo, you just looking to put a name to a face or are you looking to actually get your hands on this dude?"

Hodge's brow furrowed. "Why, you know how I can track him down?"

"The easiest way to find him is to find where his girl's band is playing. They are some loud angry metal band called Valkyrie's Revenge."

"I appreciate the tip, but given the high level shit he's into I don't know if he's going to be hitting the clubs for a concert," the Agent replied and shook his head.

"My man, you don't understand," Jimbo said slowly. "This guy is at every one of his girl's gigs. Motherfucker was three hours late with a delivery to me because he stopped by the club to watch her play. I mean this bitch ripped his nuts off and has them displayed on the mantle.

Doesn't even have the decency to put them in her purse, just right there above the fireplace. Hell, she even shows them off to her friends and everything. I know we've all had that one girl who drove us crazy, but there's being into a girl, being pussy whipped, and then there's whatever the fuck this kid is. Trust me, if his girl is playing a show, he's gonna be there."

Hodge nodded. "Thanks, Jimbo."

"Yeah yeah, I know. Just remember this shit next time I get busted."

"Consider me your get out of jail free card."

"He seems like a lovely fellow," Artemis said as he ended the call.

Hodge chuckled. "Yeah, he's not exactly the kind of guy you invite over for Thanksgiving dinner, but in a case like this he's invaluable."

She pulled up the web page for the band. "Alright, found Valkyrie's Revenge. And… damn, no shows for a couple of weeks."

He cocked his head. "What if… what if we book them? I mean doesn't Robert own one of the most famous metal bars in the city?"

She turned to him, eyebrows rising to her hairline. "So the plan is to book this band on the slight hope that they accept, Rocco the scar faced douchebag shows up and we are able interrogate him as to where Rudo is hiding?"

"Yeah I know, it's thin." He winced.

"It's anorexic ballerina thin. But it's the best we got." She sighed. "I'll make the call."

CHAPTER ELEVEN

Artemis played solitaire on the computer while Hodge paced back and forth.

"So what's the plan if the band can't play tonight?" he asked, breaking the apprehensive silence that had fallen after the phone call.

"Buy some property in the desert and build a Biodome?" She shrugged. "Pretty sure we could even get Pauly Shore to join us. He seems like the kind of guy that would do anything for money these days."

He cracked a smile, and stopped pacing to look at her. "Do me a favor, if I ever meet Brent please remind me to ask him what he was thinking by allowing Pauly Shore to have a career."

"You should have seen the guy who was popular before him. It was one of the few times I've ever requested Brent straight up murder an entertainer," she replied, spinning her chair around.

"Yikes." He winced. "He must have been unbearable."

"Just imagine the worst YouTube prankster, but with multi-million dollar budgets."

He nodded. "Sounds like justifiable homicide in my book."

Her phone trilled a ring, and she looked at the screen.

"It's Robert, so fingers crossed," she said, and answered the call. "Give me some good news, Rob."

"The girl screamed so loudly when I said I needed them to play tonight that I'm pretty sure I went deaf in one ear," he replied.

Artemis smiled. "So I'm guessing that's a yes?"

"They go on at 8. Bring earplugs."

"Thanks Robert," she said, and then ended the call. "Okay, Hodge we are on. Eight o'clock tonight."

Hodge threw his fist into the air in triumph. "Hell yeah. So what do we do in the meantime? We have eight hours to kill."

"Need to make a stop and gear up," she said.

He raised an eyebrow. "Why don't you keep your gear here?"

"You don't spend years waging a guerrilla war against the Nazi war machine in Germany and other occupied territories without adhering to the worst case scenario mentality," she explained. "By the end of the war I had dozens of safe houses and stashes set up across Europe. Been doing the same here in the States ever since I got back, some of which are better equipped than others. The stuff I keep on hand here works great for small timers like Kevin Hauser and those douchebags in the woods, but we are about to take on a much, much tougher foe."

"Makes sense to me. So where do we need to go?" he asked.

She grinned. "How do you feel about Chinese food?"

CHAPTER TWELVE

Austin was like most major cities where ethnic communities would move into a small neighborhood and make it their own. The Chinese district was just north of downtown and thrived thanks to the influx of college students from UT. Most of the stores and restaurants in this district catered to their English speaking audience by offering English language menus, however the Chinese eatery that Artemis led Hodge into did not. It didn't even have an English language sign on the outside, so it was no surprise that they were the only two Americans in the place.

A young Chinese man walked towards them and spoke in Mandarin. Hodge smiled and nodded, while Artemis nodded and responded with fluency. The Agent gaped in amazement as the two of them went back and forth for a few moments before the young man showed them to a table, handed them a menu then walked off.

"When the hell were you going to tell me you spoke Mandarin?" Hodge asked as he sat down.

She shrugged as she scanned the menu. "I can speak every language actually."

"Come again? How is that possible?" His jaw dropped.

"Some amazing future tech that came about 20 years ago," she said. "Little device about the size of a grain of rice that is implanted behind the ear, automatically translates every language and actually takes over the speech center of my brain and allows me to respond in the appropriate language."

"Do you have another one of those? That sounds amazing!" he exclaimed.

She shook her head. "Sorry, but it was custom made for me. Plus in your line of work it could very easily get you in trouble."

"How so? I would think that being able to speak the language of whoever I'm interviewing would be a huge positive."

"Well once it's implanted the translator doesn't have an off switch," she began. "So let me see if I can spell it out for you in a culturally sensitive manner as to why that's an issue. Imagine if you have to interview a couple of very enthusiastic rap fans, and they are speaking a lot of slang. What do you think their reaction would be to a middle aged white man responding in the same manner?"

"Point taken," he agreed as the waiter dropped off a duffle bag at his companion's feet. "What's this?"

"My gear," Artemis replied, not even looking up from the menu. She spoke to the waiter in Mandarin again before glancing at Hodge. "What would you like?"

He stared blankly at the menu, unable to make heads or tails of it. "Why don't you order for me? Something with chicken, please."

She rattled off something to the waiter and smiled as she handed him the menus.

"So what's in the bag?" Hodge asked.

"In due time my friend. In due time," she said with a wink. "So, you have any ideas on how to play the concert?"

He nodded. "It's going to be difficult to interrogate him in the middle of a show, so we are going to need to get him isolated. Is there a back room we could use?"

"Not really. Robert has a couple of people who work in the back room running drinks up, and it's the only pathway to the back smoking patio," she replied.

"Guess it's going to have to be the bathroom then," he groaned. "If we can get him in there during the show it should be empty, and one of us can stand guard while the other finds out where Rudo and Duke are."

Artemis shrugged. "So we just have to get a guy into the bathroom. Doesn't sound like that difficult of a task, especially when compared to everything else we've done."

"Cheers to that," he agreed, and raised his glass. They toasted as the waiter showed up with dinner, setting down a full chicken covered in a mysterious red sauce. He stared at it warily. After she tore off a leg and bit into it, he shrugged and dug in.

CHAPTER THIRTEEN

The walls of Tate's Bar shook as Valkyrie's Revenge worked their way through their first song, *Justice Through Destruction*. Artemis and Hodge approached the front door and paused to game plan.

"Robert texted me a few minutes ago and said our boy is there," she said, peering in through the front window. "It looks like a fairly packed house tonight, so we should be able to slip in without him seeing us."

He nodded. "Any ideas on how to get him to the bathroom?"

"Robert says he is hanging out near the back by the soundboard. Apparently his girl doesn't want him distracting her during the show so he can't be within her eyesight." She chuckled.

He raised an eyebrow. "She sounds like a real keeper."

"You'd be amazed what men will go through to be with a hot tattooed guitar player in a metal band," she replied. "As far as getting him back there without dragging him through the crowd and causing a commotion, I might have an idea. When we go in head to the right and go wait in the bathroom."

"You got it," he said, and then paused as he opened the door. "Hey, can I borrow your laser pen of doom? Might help with the interrogation."

She tossed it to him with a warning glance. "I want that back, just so you know."

He winked and nodded and disappeared inside.

Artemis waited a beat before following, and headed straight for the bar. Robert celebrated her arrival by sliding a glass of whiskey to her. She took a few sips and turned to check out the band, who was doing a great job of getting the crowd riled up with moshing and stage diving. On a normal night Robert would have put a stop to the diving, but there were more important things to attend to.

"Hey Robert, I need two large beers," a thirty-something blonde waitress yelled out from the counter. Her hair was pulled into a ponytail, shirt stained from multiple spilled drinks, the look in her eyes was that of a combat vet who had watched his friends blown apart by the enemy. A typical look of someone who has spent at least a decade in customer service.

The bartender nodded to her. "Coming right up."

Artemis slid over a couple of seats and took up position right beside the waitress. "Hey sweetie, you doing okay this evening?" she asked.

"Darlin' it's one of those nights. I can handle having my ass grabbed on a regular night, but this moshing bullshit is the worst when you are carrying a tray full of drinks," the waitress replied.

"Yikes, I'm sorry. I tell you what though, I think I know a way to make your evening a whole lot better."

"Honey I'll be honest, you're hot as hell but after nights like this I just don't have the energy for what you have in mind," the waitress replied as she placed the two large beers on her tray.

Artemis chuckled. "That's not quite what I had in mind. Actually, I need a small favor from you. A favor I'm willing to tip very generously for."

The waitress leaned up against the bar, ignoring her tray of drinks. "Okay, I'm listening."

"You see that guy over there next to the soundboard? The one with the face scar?" The time traveler asked, and the woman nodded, glancing across the dance floor. "He hit on me pretty hard the other night, and it turns out his girlfriend is the guitar player in the band."

"That cheating bastard. I fucking hate men like that," the waitress spat, bristling.

"Yeah, they are indeed the worst. I was hoping you could help teach him a lesson, so I thought you could baptize him with those beers there. And don't worry, Robert and I are tight, so he'll be okay with it." She pointed at the bartender who responded with a thumbs up.

"Honey, my ex cheated on me, and let me tell you, I ain't gonna stand for it. I'll douse him with beer. Hell, I'll shank his ass if you want. Make it look like an accident."

"Woah woah, dial it back hon," Artemis said as she put her hand on her new friend's shoulder to calm her. "I think the beer shower will be good enough for now. Once you soak him, tell him there are some fresh towels in the bathroom. I have a friend waiting in there to teach him a lesson."

"Oh is it a gay friend? Cause I know a guy that'll pay good money if you can get that on tape."

Artemis stared blankly at the waitress for a moment, trying to comprehend the request. After a moment they both looked over to Robert who motions for the waitress to go.

She nodded and flounced off with her tray.

"Wow," Artemis said.

Robert laughed. "Yeah, I know, but she shows up on time, works hard, and like to wear low cut tops."

"Dude, you're old enough to be her great, great, great, grandfather." She raised an eyebrow at him.

"Hey don't judge me." He put his hands up. "I own a dive bar and start drinking at nine in the morning. Being a dirty old man is just the next logical stop on my chosen life path."

She shook her head and shot back the rest of her drink as the waitress approached her target. Rocco nodded his head to the beat, oblivious to what was about to happen to him. The waitress walked by the last table between him and her and pretended to trip over the chair.

Instead of simply dropping the tray on him, she launched it several feet in an exaggerated pratfall worthy of an entry level community college improv comedy class. While she lacked style points, her aim was on target as the full contents of both beers landed squarely on Rocco.

"What the fuck you stupid bitch!" Rocco screeched, furiously wiping at his face.

"Oh my god sir, I'm so sorry," the waitress cooed. "I tripped over the chair and I, I mean, I'm just so, so sorry."

He growled. "Well don't just stand there with your head up your ass. Go get me a towel or something."

"I'm so sorry sir, but we're out of towels behind the bar. There should be plenty in the men's room however." She motioned to the general bathroom area.

"Goddamnit, you are going to make me miss my girl's set. After she's done playing I'm gonna get your clumsy ass fired," he snarled.

She feigned a terrified expression. "Oh sir, I'm so sorry, please don't."

"Just point me towards the bathroom and fuck off," he snapped.

"It's... it's down the hall over there," she stammered, and pointed.

Rocco walked off towards the men's room, still wiping the beer from his face. When he got out of range, the waitress turned towards her accomplices to give them a big thumbs up. After they responded in kind, the waitress pointed in Rocco's direction before making an inappropriate crude humping motion, insinuating that he was about to have a rough time in the john.

Artemis shook her head in disgusted amazement as Robert slid a refill her way. She downed it in a single gulp before following Rocco to stand guard at the bathroom door.

The men's room at Tate's Bar was an extension of the rest of the bar, with the walls covered in band autographs. The only difference was a giant ice filled trough and a single shoddy stall that housed a graffiti laden toilet that was missing a seat. The scar faced lackey threw open the door in anger, nearly knocking down a patron as they exited.

"That fucking bitch, I'm gonna rip her a new one," Rocco fumed as he ripped a stack of paper towels out of the holder.

Hodge stepped out of the stall and grabbed grabbed his opponent's head, smashing it forward into the mirror. The henchman cried out in shock as the Agent flung him back into the stall. The scummy toilet broke his fall, and possibly a few ribs too, if the sharp cracks were anything to go by. Before Rocco could regain his footing, his attacker was on top of him, knee in his chest.

Hodge sneered. "Remember me?"

"What? What the fuck are you doing here? You're supposed to be chained up." His prisoner gaped.

"Apparently, I'm a little more resourceful than you or your boss gave me credit for." The Agent grinned. "And you know, speaking of your boss, where is he exactly?"

"I… I don't know what you're talking about." Rocco shook his head, eyes wide.

Hodge pursed his lips. "Really? You want to play this game? Okay." He grabbed his victim's collar and flipped him over into the dreaded swirlie position. He submerged the flailing man's face into the nasty toilet water for a few moments, and then jerked him back up by the swirly hair. "As you may have noticed, this toilet has some issues. Namely it doesn't want to flush," he said as the lackey sputtered and gasped. "Judging by the look and smell, the patrons at tonight's show have been living on a steady diet of alcohol and greasy street vendor food. Not a great combination if you ask me."

"You're sick, man! You're just fucking sick!" Rocco screeched. "Oh god, I'm going to puke!"

"You might want to hold that in, unless you want to revisit it in

a few moments," Hodge warned. "*Or
you can tell me about your boss,
your choice.*"

"Okay, Okay, I'll talk!" The
now shit-covered henchman yelled.
"Okay, so his name is Rudo. He's
tall, got blonde hair. He's also a
badass mother fucker who does whatever he wants to do and there isn't
anything you can do to stop him."

Hodge laughed so long that Rocco joined him in confusion. "You're
a funny guy, you know that?" the
Agent said. "I've been known to tell
a joke from time to time, too. You
want to hear one? Oh who am I kidding, of course you do. You ready?
Knock, knock."

His victim swallowed, and reluctantly asked, "Who… who's there?"

The Agent smashed his fist into
Rocco's face, busting his nose.

"Really cop? That's all you
got? Real original," the lackey
snapped, blood coating his mouth and
chin.

Hodge pulled out Artemis's future pen of destruction. He held it

up right in front of his prisoner's face, who stopped struggling to focus on it.

"Look, I get it, you're a stupid motherfucker who is in way over their head," the Agent said, voice low and menacing. "And given your history, I'm guessing this isn't your first beating, so you probably think you can outlast me like you outlasted them. But given the look in your eyes I get the sense you know what this is and you know I'm different."

Rocco nodded, eyeing the pen with fear in his gaze.

"So, you know what happens when I do this," Hodge said, and stabbed Rocco in the arm with the pen. "And this, and this, and this!" He stabbed the lackey in the leg, chest, and head. As he hovered his finger over the detonation button, his prisoner shrieked.

"No no no no no no!" he pleaded. "Please, I'll tell you everything you want to know!"

Hodge relaxed his thumb. "I'm listening."

"You... you have to promise me you're going to let me go," Rocco stammered.

"You have my word that once you tell me what I want to know, I'm going to walk out that door and you'll never see me again."

"Okay," the lackey said with a hard swallow. "Rudo and Duke have a small building just outside of town. It's way off the beaten path and only a handful of people know about it so it's not heavily guarded."

Hodge's brow furrowed. "Then how do *you* know about it?"

"They needed my help unloading the gear. Rudo paid me, gave me a lottery number for next week and I was out the door."

"Okay, so where is it exactly?" the Agent asked.

"You know the burned out gas station on route nine headed east out of town? The one that went up in that arson a few weeks back."

"Yeah, I know it."

"It's about three miles past that. There is a dirt road on the right that will take you down into the woods. After about a mile there is a clearing with some buildings. That's where they are, I swear."

Hodge held up the pen. "Now you ain't lying to me, are you?"

"No, no! I swear, I'm telling you the truth! That's where they are, but I don't know how long they are going to be there. They were talking about moving east when I left there this morning," Rocco said, words coming out in a rush. "Oh come on man, I told you every-thing I know. You gotta keep your word. What's a man without his word, right?"

"Yeah, you're right. I'm a man of my word," Hodge said, and got to his feet. "Now, I'm going to walk out that door and you're never going to see me again. Provided that you hang tight in here for a few minutes since I gotta pay my bar tab. Can you stay in here like a good little boy?"

Rocco nodded furiously.

"I didn't quite catch that," Hodge said, holding the pen up again.

"Yes! Yes! I won't move!"

"Good boy," the Agent said as he pocketed the pen and walked out of the stall, leaving his shaking victim on the floor.

Artemis raised an eyebrow from her lean on the wall next to the bathroom door. "There you are. You find out where we need to go?"

"Yep, there is a compound just outside of town, should be lightly guarded too according to him," Hodge replied.

"Fuckin'-A," she said and clapped him on the back. "I'm impressed. How did you get it out of him? Swirly?"

"Well I started with that, but he didn't open up until I pulled this out," he explained, and produced the pen. "I didn't detonate it yet though."

"Here, allow me." She grinned as she clicked the top button. "Oh, wait, how many times did you stab him before he talked?"

Hodge shrugged. "I don't know, six, maybe seven times."

Her eyes widened. "We have to go," she urged, and grabbed his shoulder, dragging him away from the door.

"Wait, what's wrong?"

"We have to go now, and you owe Robert an apology. He likes Johnny Walker Black. Find the biggest bottle you can, and get two," she instructed.

His blood ran cold at the realization of what he had done. "Oops."

Rocco's limbs began to heat up, a tingling sensation crawling up his arms and legs.

"Oh god no," he moaned as the devices within him began to activate. He watched in horror as his flesh turned bright red, started to boil and melt off, spreading from each of the injection points. His screams would have alerted everyone to his plight if it wasn't for

Valkyrie's Revenge going into their final song, *Face Full of Lead*.

The pain spread through his body until the melting points reached each other, mixing and turning from red to blue. For a brief moment his flesh stopped melting as the blue color raced through his veins. When the blue reached the initial injection points they emitted a loud tone, as if to warn anyone nearby that they should seek cover. The tone became louder and louder, to the point where Rocco's ears began to bleed. He let out one last scream before the injections detonated, covering the graffiti walls in a fresh coat of red.

CHAPTER FOURTEEN

Artemis and Hodge parked their car a quarter mile from the clearing, not wanting to alert Rudo to their presence. She grabbed the duffel bag from the Chinese restaurant out of the back seat, threw it over her shoulder and began walking.

"You know Rudo. Any idea what we might be in for?" The Agent asked.

"If we're lucky, there won't be many guards. For all his strengths, Rudo is a lot cockier than someone in this line of work should be. He probably views me as his only real threat, and since he believes I'm out of the picture, in his mind he's already won." She rolled her eyes.

"Here's hoping you're right," he said as they reached the edge of the tree line and knelt down under cover.

The compound was a dilapidated warehouse that looked like it hadn't been used since the sixties, with peeling paint and busted out windows highlighting the neglect. A pickup truck with a gas powered generator in the back was parked beside the fuse box, producing just enough juice to illuminate the facility.

Hodge peered through his mini-binoculars and saw three figures moving boxes back and forth from the building. "I see a few men down there, but it's too dark to tell if it's Rudo or Duke," he said. "You got anything in your bag of tricks there to help out?"

"I don't believe so," she said as she rummaged. "It doesn't really matter though, as we are going to raid the place regardless if they are outside or not."

He nodded. "Okay, so what's the plan?"

"More than likely, Rudo isn't going to be doing the heavy lifting, so there's a good chance he's in the building. I'm going to sneak around and go in through the south entrance to track him down and hope that there aren't more guys inside."

Hodge raised an eyebrow. "So... what do I do?"

"Well…" Artemis cocked her head. "You see those three men down there?"

He groaned. "Well, do you at least have something in your bag that might help me survive taking on three henchmen at once? I mean I'm glad you have the utmost faith in my ability and all, but let's be realistic here."

She chuckled as she reached into the bag. She fumbled about for a few moments before pulling out a hand held water pistol.

He gaped. "Are… are you serious? Even if I was in an actual water gun fight it would be like bringing a Derringer to a bazooka battle."

"Come on, I picked you because you were bright. Did you learn nothing from my computer?" she asked as she pulled the trigger of the water gun down about halfway. A bright blue light balled at the end, with particles of white being drawn to it. Each particle that made contact with the source caused the blue light to grow larger and brighter. After a few seconds of this she released the trigger, and everything went dark again. "Hidden in plain sight, remember?"

"Holy hell that was amazing," he said as he took the weapon and inspected it closely. "Is it powerful?"

"It makes my laser pen look like a regular off the shelf pen," she explained. "You need to be careful though, because not only does that thing pack a punch, it has a sixty second cool down. So my advice is to take out a target then run like hell until it recharges."

He hung his head. "Great, more running. I swear I'm going to have to join a gym if I'm going to keep partnering with you."

"Well if you need some extreme performance enhancing drugs, just let me know. My dealer is a lot better than anyone currently alive," she replied with a wink.

He shrugged. "So where is *your* gun?"

"I'm more, shall we say, hands on," she replied as she pulled out a couple of padded sparring gloves and slid them onto her hands.

"Let me guess, they shoot missiles!" he exclaimed. "Or they teleport those you punch into a nether world dimension?"

"Nah, it's just light as a feather, hits with the power of reinforced steel, and…" She smacked the sides of her hands together, triggering a green laser bar to form over the knuckles. She demonstrated their power by punching a tree limb, slicing it clean off. "…something with a little more power should my adversary have a weapon."

He smiled then looked at his water gun. The smile dropped from his face as he realized he got the short end of the future weapon stick. "Okay, you ready to do this?"

"Once more into the breach," she agreed.

As she began to stand, he grabbed her arm. "Hey Artemis, if this goes south I just want you to know that-"

"Hodge, I swear to christ if you try and make this a sentimental moment I will stab you in the dick with my exploding pen and detonate it," she cut in.

He paled. "Oh, well, in that case—good luck, and first round is on me after we save the world."

"That's better," she said. "Now come on, world isn't going to save itself."

CHAPTER FIFTEEN

Hodge waited until the trio walked back towards the building to make his dash from the edge of the trees to the truck they were loading up. Fortunately for him, it was a long walk for them to make, giving him the necessary window to make the forty yard dash in a time that would have gotten him kicked out of the NFL combine. He crouched behind the truck to catch his breath and await their return, taking the time to psych himself up for the confrontation. A few moments passed, and he could hear the them making their way back to the truck.

"Okay guys, just a couple more trips and you'll get your payment," Duke said as they approached the truck. "You just have to figure out if you want sports scores or lotto numbers."

"Afraid that ill-gotten payday is going to have to wait," Hodge declared as he popped out from behind the truck. "Miss me, Duke?"

"Special Agent Hodge, it's good to see you again. I must admit, I am rather surprised to see you this soon." Duke raised his chin.

The Agent shrugged. "I guess that's the benefit of being me. Everyone always underestimates me, so I get to surprise people in a regular basis."

"So, here I am, the object of your obsession." The criminal spread his hands. "You know, when he re-cruited me, Rudo showed me articles on you. How you devoted so much of your life to hunting me down, always being one step behind. Must have driven you crazy to know I was out there murdering people and there wasn't anything you could do to stop me."

"Don't flatter yourself, Duke. You were nothing special. Just an-other name that came across my desk. Another low life scumbag that needed to be removed from the gene pool," Hodge replied.

"I would say whatever helps you sleep at night, but I'm just going to have my henchmen kill you so it's a non-issue." Duke motioned for the lackeys to attack. They were mirrors of each other, standing over six feet tall and ripped. If either one of them reached Hodge he knew he would be in for a bad day.

"Woah, woah, you guys just relax and listen for a moment," the Agent said, putting his hands up, palms out. The henchmen complied, much to his amazement. "I don't know who you are, nor do I care. I'm here for Duke and only Duke. You guys can take off, hitch a ride back to town, and live your life. So what do you say boys?"

"If y'all kill him I'll give you lottery numbers and a month's worth of sports scores so you can live it up in Vegas," their boss said. The two henchmen began to advance, but froze in place when their victim pulled out his gun.

He smirked. "Yeah, that's what I thought."

The standoff lasted a few seconds until Duke and the henchmen realized it was a squirt gun, which triggered uncontrollable laughing from all three of them.

Hodge chuckled as well, but kept his sights on the advancing threats. After a few moments he pulled the trigger halfway down like Artemis had shown him, creating a bright blue and ever growing light. He could feel the power coursing through the weapon, his hands trembling as they struggled to contain it. Once it became unbearable, he finished the trigger pull.

An orb of blue light rocketed out from the tip of the weapon, landing a direct hit on the lead henchmen. Everyone in the vicinity averted their eyes due to the extreme brightness. When their eyes readjusted to the darkness they saw that the upper half of the lackey had been completely eviscerated. A geyser of blood spewed forth, coating the stunned evildoers in crimson.

"Holy shit," Hodge said, and stared at the gun in disbelief. He glanced up at the other henchman wiping his face clean with his sleeve before beginning to advance. "Oh, I kind of hoped that would have scared you off."

"That was my brother motherfucker," the henchman said as he stalked forward. "I'm going to fucking *end* you."

The Agent let out a deep sigh before he took off running. The henchman yelled out as he pursued him, making up the distance between them quickly. Hodge made it about fifteen yards before his opponent caught him by the back of his shirt and jerked him backwards onto the ground. He hit the dirt with a thud and immediately scrambled to the side to get away.

"Hey look man, I'm really sorry about your brother," he said.

"Shhhhhhhhh," the man replied, holding his finger up to his lips. "You can apologize and beg all you want, but it's not going to do one damn thing to change what's about to happen to you."

"So what, you going to shoot me in the head? Get it over with quickly so you can get to mourning your brother out in Vegas?"

The henchman paused. "You know, I like that idea. Gonna get me some hoes, some top shelf liquor, and celebrate the life of my brother in style. But it can wait until after I'm done torturing your ass like you at Gitmo."

A tiny *ding* came from the gun, alerting him to the gun being recharged. He grinned. "Sorry, but I'm not really into anal play. But that's not a judgement on you. By all means, live your life."

"Man, fuck you!" the henchman yelled and darted forward. As he got into range, Hodge kicked him squarely in the knee, sending him tumbling down. The Agent caught him by the hair and pressed his body weight into his back, arching his head back.

"Open wide," he said, and rammed the water gun into the guy's mouth and pulled the trigger.

The henchman convulsed as the particles built up inside, eventually leading to the detonation of his head. The force of the blast covered Hodge in brain matter, and shattered the gun in the process.

"Fuck," he spat as he stood up and tossed the now-useless weapon aside.

"You look like you're ready for me!" Duke yelled from his position about twenty yards away.

Hodge dusted himself off and joined in the standoff. He stretched his arms out and motioned for his opponent to come on. Duke smiled before running full steam towards him. The Agent remained paralyzed at the freight train of a human being barreled towards him. Just as his opponent got into striking distance, Hodge fell straight to the ground, ducking the wrap-up attempt and tripping him up. Duke used his face to break the fall to the ground, snapping his nose in the process.

Hodge used the opportunity to make a break for the truck, in the hopes there would be a weapon he could use. Even though Duke was face down in the dirt he knew he was no match for him hand to hand, so he needed something to give him a leg up.

"Not bad, not bad at all," the now bloody-faced criminal said with a laugh as he pulled himself up from the ground. He wiped his face and looked at the crimson coating his palm. "Wow, you even drew blood. I'm impressed."

Hodge ignored him and continued to dig through the bed of the truck. He shoved away computer parts and hard drives, nothing that would allow him to fight effectively. At the sound of boots approaching, he grabbed the only thing that he could use. A broom.

"Bring it!" Hodge yelled as he held the cleaning tool out in front of him.

Duke stopped just short of him, goofy grin on his face. "What are you going to do, sweep me away?"

Hodge smiled before smacking the broom on the side of the truck, snapping the bristles away and turning it into a makeshift spear. His opponent seemed unimpressed and took a step forward, forcing the Agent to respond with a thrust.

He managed to catch Duke's left shoulder, who looked at the wound before glaring up at his attacker. Without saying a word, he lifted his giant right hand and brought it down across the center of the broom, snapping it in two.

Hodge took a step back and looked at his weapon that was now half its original size.

"That's not good," he muttered.

"No, no it isn't." Duke sneered as he pulled the broom remnant from his shoulder and tossed it aside. He cracked his neck to the side before leaping forward, leading with his fist aimed squarely at the Agent's head.

Instinctively, Hodge reacted to the incoming punch by thrusting the remaining portion of his weapon upwards, catching his attacker in the forearm. The impact wasn't enough to cause much damage, but it was enough of a shock to force his fist back. He tried to punch again, but met the same fate, a small prick to the forearm.

Duke yelled in frustration before lunging forward in an attempt to get Hodge in a bearhug. The Agent countered this move by ducking to the left and jabbing him in the side, sliding across the ground and popping up behind him and the driver side door. This only enraged him further.

Duke spun around and made another attempt to apprehend him by leading the charge with his massive fist. Hodge deftly opened up the door, so the fist made direct contact with the window, creating a spiderweb of cracks.

Before he had a chance to recover, the Agent jammed the small hunk of wood right into Duke's throat.

"Got you, you son of a bitch," he hissed as his opponent dropped to the ground, gasping for air.

Blood spurted out from the wound, coating the inside of the door as he fell to his knee. He attempted to put pressure on it in a vain attempt to prolong his life. He propped himself up by leaning on the seat, looking up with fearful eyes at the Agent standing tall above him.

"Well, I hate to cut this short but I need to go check on my friend and help her take down your boss," Hodge said as he took hold of the door with both hands. "Enjoy hell, you child killing prick," he said as he slammed the door onto Duke, driving the wood the rest of the way through his throat.

CHAPTER SIXTEEN

Artemis pried open the door to the compound, revealing a long hallway filled with broken glass and discarded furniture. Before Rudo and his crew showed up, it appeared as though this building hadn't seen human life since the Nixon administration, and judging by the destruction it wasn't a high quality form of human life.

She walked cautiously through the corridor, pausing in front of a set of double doors. She placed her ear close to them and could hear movement on the other side. She took a deep breath before she flung open the door and burst into the room.

The main room was cavernous and sparsely occupied by objects. More discarded furniture lined the walls, and the only source of recent activity was a pile of goods in the center of the room that was flanked by Rudo and tall lanky gentleman sporting a long blonde ponytail.

"Rudo!" Artemis yelled.

He and his blonde friend turned, and he chuckled as his eyes fixed on her. "I swear Artemis, once you get something in your head, not even god himself can stop you."

"Hey boss, you want me to take this bitch out?" the lanky man asked.

"It would be in your best interest to show her some respect," Rudo snapped. "She is far more capable than you are."

"Let me show you what I can do, huh?" the henchman huffed. "And when I beat her down, you give me a couple more college football scores for next week."

Rudo shook his head and shot Artemis an exasperated look. She nodded back at him, giving him the okay to set his henchman loose on her.

The blonde cracked his knuckles. "So we got a deal, or what?"

"By all means, show me what you can do," his boss replied before leaning back on the pile of goods, crossing his arms casually.

The man grinned widely before rushing towards the woman. She stood her ground, completely relaxed as he got close enough to strike. His first punch was met head on with a punch from her, and the force of the blow from the future weapon fist shattered his hand. He stumbled back with a yelp, staring in shock at his now useless hand.

"You can run along now little man," she taunted. "I'm through with you."

Undeterred, the blonde pulled a knife with his good hand. Artemis, unimpressed, smacked it out of his hand before punching him in the chest. He landed with a thud on his back, dazed.

"You really should have listened to your boss over there." She sneered, standing over him like a lion over its prey. "You could have lived to see another day."

"No no no, please… please don't kill me," the man pleaded.

"Sorry, you had your chance," she said with a shrug. "I gotta save the world, and I can't risk you getting another thought in your head that you can take me out when I'm not looking." She slammed the side of her hands together, triggering the laser knuckles. "If you come back in your next life as a bigger piece of shit, here's hoping you remember this lesson," she said before punching him directly in the throat. The laser cut through his flesh like it was nothing, completely detaching his head from the rest of his body.

Artemis stood up, powered off the laser, and kicked the head over to the side before turning her attention back to Rudo. "Come on, is that the best you got? He wasn't much of a challenge."

"An entire Nazi platoon wasn't much of a challenge for you, so what chance did this asshole have?" Rudo rolled his eyes. "I swear, it's good to see you in action again. Even after what—seventy, eighty years?—you are still at the top of your game."

She shrugged. "Well to be fair, I haven't taken much time off since the war."

"Which is precisely the reason why I left you alive," he said. "You do amazing work saving innocent lives while punishing the guilty. You're like an R-rated superhero that rights wrongs before they can even take place. I want—no I *need*—people like you in my America."

"That's exactly why I'm here, to save innocent lives," she said, eyes sad.

"Why don't you trust me?" he asked with a sigh. "You know more than anyone that making this country great is more important to me than anything. I even sacrificed my family to protect it! I… I killed them all to protect this secret, this power, and I'm not going to let them die in vain. I'm going to use this technology to its fullest potential and make this country the most powerful nation today, tomorrow, and for all time!"

"I'm sorry that your family is gone," she said sincerely. "I'm sorry that you had to do what you did, but perverting our mission isn't the way to honor them. Our mission was to prevent America from being destroyed, and we succeeded far beyond our wildest dreams. When we were back at the bunker, waiting for the machine to power up again we would sit and talk about what we thought we could accomplish, do you remember that?"

He nodded with a small smile. "I seem to remember our pie in the sky, best case scenario was to sabotage Germany to the point where Russia could overrun them and the rest of Europe. It would have doomed tens of millions to authoritarian rule, but our nation would have been a little better off and there wouldn't have been a nuclear war that decimated the planet. Little did we know, huh?"

"Yep, we went from marginally better to a world superpower in the blink of an eye. But instead of being happy with that, you want to play god and destroy not just us, but the entire world," she said.

His brow furrowed. "What are you talking about?"

"Have you not looked into your own future?" She threw her hands up. "Six years from now, you run a successful Presidential campaign, then about two months in you decide it's time to let the world in on your little secret. Rather than make the country untouchable, it unites the rest of the world against us, and try as you might, you aren't able to prevent a global nuclear war. Every country, not just America, gets wiped from existence."

"Artemis, Artemis, Artemis." He put up a hand. "You are just seeing the first draft of things to come. Don't you remember during the war? There were several times when total annihilation was predicted, and we prevented it from happening every single time."

"This is different and you know it," she hissed. "We played our

cards close to our chest back in
those days, so nobody knew what we
were capable of. The moment you reveal to the world you can see into
the future it all comes crashing
down. No leader, no nation is going
to let you have that kind of power."

He raised his chin. "We shall
see."

"No, we won't," she replied
softly. "You are a dear friend, a
brother in arms. I have risked life
and limb to save you, and we have
killed untold numbers of men together in pursuit of a better world. But
as you always say, the mission comes
first. Right now you are the biggest
threat to the country and the
world."

"I'm sorry you see it that
way." He clenched his jaw. "I'm going to give my family a country they
would have been proud to live in,
even if it means ending you." He
straightened his shoulders and
flipped open the lid to one of the
boxes. He pulled out a large metal
baton, about four feet in length and

the diameter of a baseball. "Before we begin, I just want you to know this isn't personal. I just have to do right by my family."

"I understand." She nodded. "The feeling is mutual."

They stared at each other for one more moment, before loosening into fighting stances with a nod.

Rudo strode over and swung the bar like a slugger going for a home run. Artemis jumped back to avoid the blow before leaping forward to take advantage of his backswing momentum. She was able to land a punch on the back of his arm, forcing him to release the bar. As it clanged to the ground, he spun around and shoved her forward a few feet. She turned back to a defensive stance and waited for him to pick up the bar again.

"You always did prefer speed over power, didn't you?" he asked as he readied himself for the next salvo.

She shrugged. "Well in my view it's better to take three guys out quickly rather than one guy out via overkill."

"That is a sound strategy, when you aren't in one on one battles like this." He sneered.

"We'll see, old friend," she said before banging the side of her right hand on her head, triggering the laser knuckles on that hand only.

Artemis made the first move, lunging towards him as he swung the pole. She made direct contact with the bludgeon about 8 inches from the top, severing it with her laser fist. Rudo spun completely around and came back with another swing which met the same fate, another 8 or so inches shaved off.

He took a quick hop back to inspect the damage done to his weapon, which was now not much longer than baseball bat. He raised the club above his head and struck downwards, which she deftly avoided by side-stepping and thrusting down with her enhanced arm. She hit the bar at an angle, shearing the pipe in half but also into a pointed shiv.

Rudo pulled back and prepared another strike. He lunged forward with the tip of the weapon aimed right at head level. Artemis leaned back to avoid being hit, and punched upwards with the laser knuckles, striking him on the wrist. His hand continued forward and to the ground as he pulled back his nub in pain. He gaped at his missing appendage for a moment before snarling and attempting a fighting stance again. But soon the shock set in as blood poured down his arm and he fell to one knee.

"It's over Rudo," she said as she deactivated her fists.

"Artemis!" Hodge yelled as he entered the room. He quickly ran over to her side and let his guard down once he saw the situation was well in hand. "Are you okay?"

"Yeah, I'm fine," she said, unlatching the gloves to remove them. "Grab that dead guy's shirt and bandage Rudo up."

"What? Why?" The Agent asked, brow furrowed in frustration.

She raised her chin. "Because I'm not killing him yet. I'm going to give him a choice."

Hodge shook his head in disbelief before he complied with the request. "One of these days you are going to have to tell me the full story of what you two did in Germany. Maybe then this will make sense."

Rudo collapsed to the ground, the reality of his failed plan sinking in, and tears began to well up. "I've… I've failed. I let down my family, they… they died for nothing."

"It's okay big guy," Hodge said in an attempt to calm him down so he could begin to dress the wound. "Here, let me take care of this."

Artemis sat beside then and put her hand on her ex-companion's back. "I know it's difficult. It's never easy losing someone you care about. I'm not going to pretend to know what it's like to be the cause of that loss, and while I'm sympathetic to your pain I also can't pretend you didn't do horrible things in order to avenge them. So, I'm going to give you a choice. It's not going to be a pleasant one mind you, but it's better than killing you outright."

He nodded jerkily. "Okay, let's hear it. My fate is in your hands."

"There is a town about 50 miles from here," she explained. "Incredibly small, backwoods, but large enough to have a decent grocery store and a few other luxuries. I purchased some property there a while back and converted it into a safe house of sorts. It's nothing fancy, but it's a lot better than death or a prison cell.

"But don't let those comforts fool you, this will be your prison. You will be cut off from all future tech, outside of the new hand I'm going to make for you and a carefully curated selection of movies and TV shows that I bring you. You will be injected with both a tracker, and a detonator to make sure you don't leave the designated area I set for you. This may or may not be permanent, but it will be a safe bet to plan on being there for a long, long while."

He reluctantly lifted his nub into the air, holding it for a second before realizing his hand wasn't there. "Sorry, I was attempting to give you a thumbs up."

"Okay Hodge, let's get loaded up and get out of here," Artemis said. "If memory serves, you owe me a drink."

CHAPTER SEVENTEEN

Artemis and Hodge walked into the office and tossed their gear to the ground. Artemis collapsed in her computer chair while Hodge perches on the edge of the desk.

"Well, that was quite the little adventure there," he said with a tired smile. "I don't even know how I'm going to explain why I'm not going to keep working on the Duke case to my boss."

"Just give me a few weeks so I can stage the compound," she replied. "Gonna make it look like he went on a rampage and was taken out by his own men. I'll call it in anonymously but make sure the tip sounds crazy enough that nobody except for you will go looking for it. You get the credit, clear your case and are off to bigger and better things."

"Yeah," he said thoughtfully. "I think that would work just fine. Thank you."

She shrugged. "Consider it my way of thanking *you* for helping me save the world."

"Well, I was kind of hoping for some lottery numbers, but I guess this will do." He grinned.

"Now now Hodge, gotta save something for your birthday," she replied with a wink.

He laughed. "So, now what?"

"What do you mean?" She raised an eyebrow.

"Are we still going to work together? Are you going to use some sort of future ray and wipe my memory clean?" he asked. "Or worse?"

"For starters don't worry, I'm not going to go all Rudo on you," she assured him. "I think you understand what possessing your knowledge means, and I'm pretty sure you've seen me in action enough to know you'd never be able to take me in a fight, so you don't want to press your luck."

"Well that's a relief."

"But to fully answer your question, yes, we can certainly work together," she continued. "I've been working solo for so long, this was a nice reminder that it's good to have a partner every now and then. I gotta warn you though, I have a high motor and run through more cases than you can imagine, so you'll need to be on your toes to keep up."

"I'm game. Just... not today," Hodge replied. "I'm already going to have a tough enough time explaining to my wife where I've been the past few days."

Artemis laughed. "Don't worry, I'll be in touch."

"Phone call this time, no laser carvings into maniac's chests," he said with a smile.

"Anybody ever tell you that you take the fun out of everything?"

"I've heard that a few million times in my life."

They chuckled and headed for the door.

"Okay, go home, get some rest," she instructed.

"You get some rest too," he shot back, and then waved before closing the door behind him.

Artemis walked back to her desk, picked up an eraser and cleared the President's board. She picked up a marker with her other hand and marked out Duke's name before pausing.

She took a long look at the *Saved* board. She thought for a minute before erasing the number and writing *EVERYONE*. She smiled at that sight as her computer beeped with an alert. Before responding to it she added a plus sign below *EVERYONE*.

She nodded. "Looks like it's time to start a new counter."

END